Playing With Fire

Alison Rose knows there's two things she can always count on:

1. Cousin Kelly – she's her best friend. They'd do *anything* for each other.
2. The fact that everyone else in her family will stop at nothing to destroy each other.

But maybe, just maybe, Alison's got one of ⎯⎯⎯ wrong.

⎯⎯⎯ing is full of surprises…

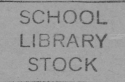

LOOK OUT FOR:

The Mystery Girl
On the Edge

Little Secrets

Playing With Fire

Emily Blake

■SCHOLASTIC

For Craig Walker,
an excellent keeper
of little secrets

First published in the UK in 2007 by Scholastic Children's Books
An imprint of Scholastic Ltd
Euston House, 24 Eversholt Street, London, NW1 1DB, UK
Registered office: Westfield Road, Southam, Warwickshire, CV47 0RA
SCHOLASTIC and associated logos are trademarks and or registered
trademarks of Scholastic Inc.

First published in the US by Scholastic Inc, 2006
Text copyright © Emily Blake, 2006
The right of Emily Blake to be identified as the author of this work
has been asserted by her.
Cover illustration copyright © Nicola Slater, 2007

10 digit ISBN 0 439 94298 5
13 digit ISBN 978 0439 94298 0

A CIP catalogue record for this book is available from the British Library

Printed by CPI Bookmarque, Croydon, Surrey
Papers used by Scholastic Children's Books are made from wood grown in
sustainable forests.

1 3 5 7 9 10 8 6 4 2

www.scholastic.co.uk/zone

There were only two things Alison Rose knew she could count on: her best friend and cousin, Kelly, and the fact that everyone else in her family would stop at nothing to destroy one another.

Like now. Alison was in the middle of a battle with her made-of-steel mother. And this time she was not going to lose. Digging her orange-painted nails into her palms, she lobbed a verbal grenade.

"It's not like I expect you to come to anything I do," Alison said. After fifteen years she knew better than that. She took a breath and did her best to keep her voice steady. If she lost her temper, her mother would refuse to discuss it any further. Full stop. "But I can't miss this game," she said evenly. "It's the championship. The last game of the season. Besides, people are relying on me – I'm part of a team."

Halfway across the living room, Helen Rose sat in the wingback chair wearing her sky-blue cashmere bathrobe – the one that matched her eyes. Her short auburn hair was perfectly styled after a long day of work. It always was. After all, her illustrious career as a domestic trendsetter was based on being perfectly styled.

"Teams are for people who don't have the ability to get anywhere on their own," Helen replied. She did not bother to look up from her laptop. It was a tactic Alison knew she used on her employees when she wanted them to feel insignificant. But Helen underestimated her daughter: Alison was tougher than your usual CEO's assistant – and better trained.

"Or for people who know how to co-operate," Alison shot back smoothly.

Helen's eyes remained fixed on the computer screen, but Alison saw her face tighten. "I don't see why I should let you use the driver on Saturday when you're too busy to make an appearance with me on Sunday," she stated calmly. "After all, the book signing is a good opportunity for both of us." She checked her manicure and waited for Alison to comply like she usually did.

There was no way. Not this time. First of all, Alison did not work for her mother. Second, she was not about to miss the championship game. And third, she was sick and tired of playing the happy daughter at her mother's endless string of events.

"If you are so anxious for us to look like a normal family, maybe you should try acting like a normal mother, *Honey*."

Alison knew her mother despised her real name, along

with just about everything else Alison's grandmother Tamara Diamond had given her. Helen and Tamara had stopped speaking long ago – before Alison was born. Warm and fuzzy mother–daughter relations did not run in the Diamond family.

When Helen finally turned and looked Alison in the face, Alison could see the crow's feet around her light eyes. She'd landed a hit. The wound was open – time for the salt. "I'm already going to a 'family' event on Sunday anyway. Why don't you tell your fans and TV crews that I'm at Grandmother's? You haven't forgotten her birthday, have you?" Alison's fingers uncurled as she gained the upper hand. Her mother pretended not to be bothered, but Alison could tell by her flaring nostrils that she was . . . and that she was calculating her next move.

Alison braced herself. It wasn't like she enjoyed this. What she wanted more than anything else was a normal life. A mother who cared about her. A father who bothered to show up. A family that got along . . . and didn't own half the town.

Helen was silent as she struggled behind her mask of calm. She didn't like to be reminded that she was the one who was too busy for Alison and not the other way around. More than that, she hated any reference to the Diamond/Rose family feud. The severed ties were a nasty blemish on Helen's otherwise perfect appearance. And Helen Rose cared about nothing more than appearances.

She had, quite literally, written the book on it: *Helen Rose's Looking Good*. The book had made her a household name, along with her magazine and the hundreds of *Looking Good* household items available at a fine retailer near you.

She'd just love to stick me *on a shelf,* Alison thought. All too often she felt like one of her mother's products – stamped with Helen's name and her "busy" bumblebee emblem – made to "look good". But Alison knew there was a big difference between looking good and feeling good.

Breathing through her nose, Helen slid her reading glasses back on and peered once again at her laptop. She was finished arguing and was now doing what she called "getting busy". It was what she did whenever she didn't want to deal with something, especially her daughter.

Ding. Alison had won the round, even if she hadn't really managed to win her mother's attention.

"So, I can take the limo?" Alison drummed her fingernails on the marble mantel and watched her mother turn away, as if Alison were dragging her nails down a chalkboard. Alison knew she could have the car. She just wanted to hear Helen say it.

She never would. At that moment the doorbell rang, followed by a pounding on the perfectly painted autumn-rust door. Helen turned her glare towards the noise – there was no way she was going to answer it.

Sighing, Alison went to the front hall. The pounding continued.

"One second!" she yelled.

Then she looked through the peephole and saw what looked like the entire FBI outside, lights flashing.

Chapter 2

The next few minutes passed so quickly that Alison felt like they took place in the space of a single gasp. She opened the door. Badges were flashed. Someone asked where her mother was.

Alison couldn't move. She couldn't speak. She didn't tell them. (She hoped her mother knew this.) But the officers came in anyway. One of them even said, "Excuse me," as she passed. Finally Alison managed to wrap her brain around what was happening. She followed the officers back to the living room just in time to see her mother being read her rights.

"You have the right to remain silent."

As if.

"Anything you say can be used against you in a court of law—"

Helen Rose interrupted the officer. She was not about to remain silent. Besides, rules hardly ever applied to her. "What do you think you're doing?" she asked incredulously. "Get your filthy hands off me."

Alison looked from her mother to the officers. She could

see that Helen Rose wasn't going to be able to bully her way out of this one. The expressions on the officers' faces were not exactly friendly – or submissive.

"Do you have any idea who I am?" Helen demanded.

"Yes, ma'am. We do," a man in a dark suit replied flatly. "Now, I'm afraid you'll have to come with us." He flashed a warrant. "The press will probably be here in a matter of minutes, so the faster we get you out of here, the better it will be for everyone."

"You have *got* to be kidding." Helen raised her chin slightly and stared venomously at the man holding the handcuffs. "She's behind this, isn't she? *She's* done it, right down to alerting the media. But mark my words, Officer –" Helen leaned in and read a name off the officer's name tag – "Griffith, she won't get away with it. Not this time."

Who in the world is Mother talking about? Alison's mind was in an uproar. She couldn't process what was going on. *She who?* Helen certainly had plenty of enemies, but none powerful enough to have her arrested. Right? Then the more obvious question hit Alison square in the face: *What has my mother done?*

Officer Griffith seemed as baffled as Alison about who Helen was accusing. "I'm not sure what you mean, Mrs Rose. We're here to conduct a thorough investigation. You are being charged with embezzlement, grand larceny and tax fraud. Now, I need you to come with me as quickly as you can. We can do it with cuffs or without. What's your choice?"

Helen glared at the officer. "You are making the biggest mistake of your life." She pushed past him, ignoring the dangling cuffs. "I'm calling my lawyer." Grabbing her mobile, she pushed a single button. When she got voice mail she snorted impatiently and snapped the phone shut.

Alison's heart hammered in her chest as she stared at the scene in front of her. Part of her wanted to scream at these intruders, to tell them to get out of her house and let her mom go. But another part wanted them to take her mother away and throw the book at her for . . . everything . . . anything. Just take her away.

No, she thought. *Stop it. She's your mother.*

She looked at all the waiting officers. With their polyester-blend uniforms and leather-holstered guns, they looked completely out of place in Helen Rose's extravagantly furnished mansion. The handmade carpet they were standing on probably cost more than two of them made in a year. This was a big catch for them, and they knew it. She could see some of the officers looking around, checking out the Italian marble mantelpiece, the twelfth-century English chest, the state-of-the-art stereo designed to fade into the background – to fill the room with sound but not distract from the custom leather couches. Just like everyone else who hovered around Helen Rose, the officers who had come to arrest her probably hoped her fame and wealth would rub off on them, if only for a minute or two.

Too bad for you it's not contagious, Alison thought. *Just genetic.*

Still trying to control the situation, Helen's ice-blue eyes scanned the room and finally fell upon Alison.

"Alison," she said, reaching her arm out affectionately.

Despite her touching display, Alison knew that until that second her mother had forgotten all about her.

"I can't possibly leave my daughter!" Helen gasped.

"We'll make sure she's taken care of," the lead officer said. "Someone will watch her while we search. Now it's time for you to go."

He nodded, and dark-clad officers swarmed around Helen like ants on a dying snail. Alison could only stare as they branched out, heading down the hall towards the kitchen and up the main staircase to the bedrooms . . . including hers.

"Mom, what are they doing?" Alison felt totally vulnerable. "Why is this happening? What have you done?" The whole house was being overtaken. But Helen stood perfectly erect, wrapped in her soft cashmere, surrounded by police and wincing at the panic in her daughter's voice.

Alison just watched as Officer Griffith steered Helen towards the door. "Call your father. He'll need to arrange bail," Helen instructed. Then she was gone and another officer was telling Alison that everything was going to be OK, and she should just sit down. Alison barely heard. It was happening too fast. Her mother was being taken away.

Words like *prison* and *indictment* were being used. Officers were going through files, moving artwork, looking for hiding places. Alison staggered back and landed on the sofa, knocking off the meticulously arranged pillows.

Bail? The word hung in Alison's head, making her think of a sinking ship. Was that it? Her mother was done fighting? Did that mean she was guilty? Of what?

Alison felt like the water was closing over her head as she watched the scene in her driveway through the picture window. Still holding the warrant, Officer Griffith led her mother to a black sedan. He opened the door to the back seat and guided Helen inside with a hand on the top of her head. It was just like a movie – like some cop film her aunt Christine would be in. But this wasn't Aunt Christine, it was her mom. And it wasn't a movie.

"Where is your father? Does he live here?" a female officer asked.

Good questions. "Yes, he lives here." Alison heard her voice like it was coming from outside her body. "He's probably at the country club bar," she mumbled, not even bothering to hide the truth.

"You should call him," the officer said gently. So Alison did. He freaked out immediately, of course. He demanded she pass the phone to the officer, who told him where Helen had been taken. Then he hung up without another word to his daughter.

"Don't worry, I'm fine," Alison whispered to herself. She

closed her eyes and listened to the officers tearing her house – her life – apart. She overheard one officer telling another that all of the Rose accounts – personal and business – had been frozen pending investigation, and that Helen's offices were also being searched at that very moment.

Alison opened her eyes and saw officers carrying file boxes and other personal items outside to a big black van. The last guy had her mother's Coach bag.

"Hey, Frank," he called to another officer. "Am I *Looking Good*?" He slung the pink leather bag in the crook of his elbow and pulled a Helen Rose magazine cover pose. His laugh died in his throat when he saw Alison staring right at him. "Sorry about that," he said contritely as he passed her. Alison wished she had a quick retort that would leave him reeling. Her mother would have.

"Don't listen to them," the nice officer said. "Do you want to call anyone else before your dad gets home? You can call anyone you want. You don't have to go through this alone."

Alison was struck dumb by the tiny show of compassion and nodded stupidly. Call somebody. She stared at her tiny silver mobile phone and flipped it open.

Her first thought was of her boyfriend, Chad. But his father confiscated his phone at nine every night and didn't give it back until the morning. Even in emergencies. Besides, she wasn't sure she was ready to talk to him about *this* yet.

Call someone, Alison thought. She stared at the screen on her phone – it showed a picture of two girls, one with dark hair, one with light. They were grinning widely with their faces pressed together.

Alison's hands were shaking uncontrollably now. She hit the voice ID button and choked out the name of the only person she could talk to right now, her cousin – her best friend.

"Kelly."

Chapter 3

Kelly Reeves flipped open her cell without even looking to see who was calling. It would be Alison. It always was. Not that that was a problem, just . . . standard. Kelly laughed to herself before she even said hello. As much as her cousin tried to deny it, Alison was Helen Rose's daughter through and through. Scheduled. Perfect. Poised. Predictable. Any other mother's dream come true. Including Kelly's mom's. The thought chafed a little under the straps of her silk tank top. Maybe it was time to stir things up.

"Hey, Al. What's up?" Kelly asked without taking her eyes from her giant flat-screen TV. Her cousin probably wanted advice on what to wear the next day. She could never come up with ideas to irritate her mother on her own, and Kelly always had lots of suggestions. But that wasn't it tonight.

"Kelly!" Alison sounded totally freaked. "They took my mom. They took her! She's gone!"

"What?" Kelly asked, sitting up on her king-sized bed. "Slow down." This sounded juicy. She needed details. She hit the mute button on the remote, killing the surround sound so she could hear the full story. "Take a deep breath," she advised, "and tell me what happened."

"The cops – I mean, the FBI. Someone. They stormed in and arrested Mom. Searched the whole house and took a bunch of stuff. They said they were searching her offices, too. And had frozen her accounts. Oh, Kel – this is so awful. Mom was still in her bathrobe."

Kelly thought she heard a sob. She bit her lip to keep from smiling. Helen Rose arrested in her pyjamas? This was better than juicy. This sounded like full-scale humiliation.

"Oh, Alison, what did she say?" Kelly filled her voice with concern, then leaned down to blow on her newly painted toenails. "Frostbite", her signature colour.

"She told me to call Dad, so he could arrange bail. Bail, Kelly! My mom's in *prison*." Alison was clearly freaking out. Typical.

"Alison, listen to me," Kelly said sternly, pulling back her Kate Spade duvet. "Your mom will be fine. She's Helen Rose. No way can they keep her in jail. Your dad will get her out, and all of this will get cleared up. Your job is to stay calm. You've got to keep it together."

"But. . ."

"But nothing. You have to think positive. Somebody probably framed your mom, and when we find out who it is, she'll get off and they'll pay. That's how it works in our family. If we're crossed, somebody pays."

Alison sniffed loudly and Kelly pulled the phone away

from her ear. Gross. "Are you all right?" Kelly asked more softly.

"Yes, I think so," Alison replied. Her voice sounded shaky but relatively normal.

"Do you want me to come over there? Where's Elise?" Kelly knew it was the housekeeper's day off, but she hoped Elise was at the house anyway. She really didn't want to go anywhere. Her toenail polish was still tacky, and she was already in her pyjamas. But if her cousin really needed her. . .

"She's off today. But I'm fine, really," Alison said with a sniffle. "Dad will be home any minute. He'll know what to do."

That was doubtful. They both knew it was the women in the Diamond family who handled everything. But Kelly didn't say so. "Well, call me back if you need to. I'll leave my phone on all night."

"I will. Thanks, Kelly. I'll see you tomorrow."

"'K, bye." Kelly hung up and hit the mute button again. She quickly flipped over to CNN.

"Whoa," Kelly whispered as she stared at an overhead shot of the Rose estate. Helicopters were swarming the place like wasps at a barbecue. Searchlights were everywhere. This was big, even by Diamond standards. And Alison was inside, all alone.

By the time the Rose coverage was over, Kelly's nails were dry and she was dying to discuss the news. She pulled out the foam toe-separators and tossed them in the wastebasket. She thought she heard her mom getting ready for bed across the hall. For a moment she thought about telling her mother what was going on, but she could not face the concern on her mom's face when she found out about her favourite niece's plight. "Poor little Alison" would get plenty of sympathy soon enough.

Flopping belly-down across her bed, Kelly checked the clock. 10.01. Definitely not too late to call Aunt Christine in California. This news was just too fabulous to keep to herself.

Chapter 4

The next few days were a nightmare. Reporters. Cameras. Alison couldn't leave the house – and her mother couldn't leave jail, because all the Rose accounts really had been frozen by the IRS. The second-richest woman in Silver Spring could not post bail and was too proud to ask her family for help.

Weirder, Alison's relationship with Chad seemed to be frozen, too. She'd called him first thing Thursday morning, then realized he was already at school, where she couldn't bear to go. He called back later that night, but Alison and her dad were getting a legal pep talk from her mother's lawyers. When *that* nightmare finally ended it was too late to call back. And then the next day Chad didn't call at all. Alison looked at her mobile screen every thirty seconds, checking for new calls, but . . . nothing.

There was no way she was going to her volleyball game now. She didn't even care if they won or lost. She wasn't ready to be seen in public.

Kelly was Alison's only lifeline. And it was Kelly who told Alison that as much as she might want to, she couldn't skip

Grandmother Diamond's birthday party, which was going on as planned, despite (or was it because of?) all the media attention.

"You have to go. How would it look if you didn't? It would be practically announcing your mom is guilty. I mean, you don't have anything to be ashamed of. Right?" Kelly's voice was starting to break up on the bad mobile connection, but Alison knew she was right.

"OK," she agreed. "But only if I can find something decent to wear." She hoped shopping would make her feel more normal. Something had to.

"Of course." Kelly practically laughed. "I guess you need a ride, huh? Be there in forty-five."

Did Kelly sound annoyed? It was a pain not having the driver any more. Or any privacy. Alison peeked around her mom's velvet curtains before she got ready. There were still a few reporters camped outside the gates. Her dad had tried to run them off a couple of times, but they took him about as seriously as her mom did – not at all.

"I can't let it get to me. I can't let any of it get to me," Alison whispered to herself as she applied her favourite gloss and picked out her biggest, darkest sunglasses. Hiding behind them, she felt a little like her mother, and Grandmother Diamond, too. They lived their whole lives behind big facades. Funny how they were so alike and *so* could not stand each other. Suddenly a new thought occurred to Alison: did they hate each other because they were the same?

When Kelly's family's big black SUV pulled into the drive, Alison ran out and jumped inside. She slid into the back next to her cousin and slammed the door, happy to have tinted windows between her and the reporters' camera lenses.

"So, I'm thinking sequins," Kelly said seriously as her driver, Tonio, accelerated through the automatic gate, away from the house. She was acting like nothing was wrong. Like the paparazzi on the lawn was nothing new.

"Wouldn't Her Highness love that?" Alison asked, using the nickname she and Kelly had created for their grandmother when they were little. Sequins at an afternoon event – how gauche. The look of horror on Grandmother Diamond's face would be priceless. Kelly could pull that kind of stunt. Alison didn't dare.

"'Course, it doesn't really matter what *you* wear," Kelly said as they sped down the wide road, past tree-lined drives and newly built, gated mansions designed to look old. "Her Highness would adore you if you showed up in bike leathers."

Alison laughed. She thought she heard a tiny kernel of jealousy in Kelly's words. It was true that Grandma D was not as hard on her as she was on Kelly. But so what? She hoped Kelly wasn't going to get in one of her moods over it. Kelly's moods were often stormy, unpredictable, and really chilly. Right now she needed some *good* Alison-and-Kelly time. Behind the tinted windows in the dark cave of the car, laughing with her best friend, Alison was beginning to feel more like herself than she had in days, and she wasn't going to let anyone spoil it.

"That's it!" Kelly took one glance at Alison's outfit as she came out of the dressing room. "That's definitely it."

Alison twirled in front of the mirrors, letting the gauzy, pale fabric of the skirt swish around her legs. Kelly was right, as usual. Of the five things she'd tried, this was definitely the one.

"Now let's get out of here." Kelly stood up and grabbed her bag. "Get changed."

Alison did one more spin, studying the breezy Betsey Johnson broomstick skirt and cute Vivienne Tam top before going back into the dressing room. She did not doubt the outfit, but she was stalling. She didn't want to go home. Just the thought was too depressing.

"Where to now?" Alison asked her cousin, plunking her platinum credit card on the counter.

"Home, I guess." Kelly yawned and ran her hand through her straight blonde hair. "I have some school stuff to do."

That was the answer Alison was afraid of. She tried to think of something, anything else she could lure Kelly to do. But Kelly was already paging Tonio.

"Sorry, Miss, your card was declined. Would you like to try another or pay with cash?" The salesperson behind the counter didn't sound sorry. He sounded annoyed as he handed Alison's card back.

Alison gulped. She looked in her lime-green clutch. She barely had enough cash for a latte. And if the platinum card was declined, her others were probably no good, either. Duh. Why hadn't she realized that her cards would be frozen along with her mother's accounts?

"Umm." Alison turned to Kelly. Her face was flaming hot. So much for feeling normal.

"I got it." Kelly reached for her own wallet, but Alison stopped her.

"Never mind." Alison flipped the edge of the fun boho skirt like she was brushing off a fly. She could not bring herself to look Kelly or the salesguy in the eye. "I can wear my Prada blazer with tuxedo pants." She hoped she sounded like she didn't care as she walked off, leaving the clothes and her pride on the counter.

Chapter 5

The next day Alison stepped out of her dad's car on to her grandmother's walk. Jack Rose had looked completely put out when she'd asked for the ride. He wasn't used to having to do anything for his daughter – or having anything to do with his mother-in-law. He didn't say a single word on the way. Alison wasn't sure if she should be mad or grateful for the silence. But the longer it lasted, the more bitter she got. It wasn't her fault they couldn't even afford a cab now. Heaven forbid her own father should have to get dressed and leave the house or acknowledge her in any way. Even now, as she turned around to thank him, he just lifted his hand, brushing her off before pulling out in front of a stretch Hummer and zooming away from the Diamond estate.

"Bye," Alison mumbled, shaking her head. *Out of the frying pan,* she thought.

Taking a deep breath, she ignored the flashbulbs and the shouted questions of the reporters outside the gates as she walked up to the three-storey brick mansion. The pillared porch was wide and covered in enormous stone pots spilling blooms. The lawns were so well clipped and raked they looked vacuumed. From the outside the Diamond estate looked very kempt and fairly welcoming . . . if you didn't know what lay inside.

Polite chatter and congratulations drifted through the massive open door. The guests were dressed to the hilt and lining up to get inside. The receiving line was so slow, waiters in short white coats were serving drinks to the guests still waiting on the porch.

Tamara Diamond's seventieth birthday party was the event of the year. No surprise – Tamara Diamond was the most powerful and least loved woman in Silver Spring. She owned half the town.

And probably more than half the guests, Alison thought. The list of one hundred invitees had been carefully created and edited . . . and edited some more until it included only the most important and influential people. Kelly was right, Alison realized. She couldn't miss this. But she could barely face it, either.

Tugging her silk camisole down and pushing her big sunglasses higher on her nose, Alison tried to steel herself the way Helen would. She knew her family would be full of fake concern, prying for details and gloating all the while. It had really burned them that after Helen Rose was written out of Her Highness's will she had – without looking back – gone on to make her own sizable wad of cash. And as much as Alison resented her mom for spending every waking moment doing just that, she didn't want to give the

Diamonds the satisfaction of seeing Helen's family breaking down because she was in jail. Even if it was.

At least Kelly will be here, Alison thought. Kelly always seemed to navigate the family politics with ease. Sometimes Alison felt like Kelly was her Diamond family tour guide. How she managed to slip past all the barbs and daggers unscathed, Alison had no idea. Perhaps the thorns did not hurt her. Or maybe she was better at hiding it. Regardless, Kelly was always there for her. Well, almost always. And Alison was there for Kelly, too. It had been that way since they were tiny. Alison could remember hiding under the table with Kelly, eating Jordan almonds out of the crystal bowl they'd nicked from the buffet and giggling at the runs in the grown-ups' panty hose while Grandmother and the aunts argued above them. Just thinking of Kelly made Alison feel stronger. She took a deep breath and walked through the door.

"Alison!" Tamara's youngest daughter, Christine, spotted Alison and practically dragged her inside. She threw her arms around her niece and pulled her against her inflated chest. "You poor thing. How are you?"

"Hi, Aunt Christine." Alison pulled away from the embrace and the phony sympathy. "I didn't know you were coming. I thought you were on location."

The actress flipped her perfectly highlighted blonde on blonde hair off her shoulder. "Oh, doll. When I heard about your mom I knew I couldn't stay away."

Your mother's seventieth birthday wasn't a good enough reason to fly in, but my mother's arrest was? Alison smiled at her aunt. It was just like her to show up to revel in misery – especially somebody else's. *She's probably hoping she can get some publicity out of it,* Alison thought bitterly. Christine was not getting the attention or movie offers she once had. The roles she used to command were going to women in their twenties. Sure, Aunt Christine looked great for her age, as long as you didn't look too closely. Hollywood demanded youth but added years.

Christine was definitely here for publicity, Alison decided. Her aunt rarely did anything for anyone other than herself. And Alison couldn't remember the last time Christine and Helen had even been on speaking terms.

Looking over her aunt's shoulder, Alison saw Grandmother Diamond in the three-storey foyer surrounded by guests. They were all cooing and fawning despite the fact that the old woman looked thoroughly bored. She had taken the time to dress in her best white Armani suit and Tiffany diamonds, the ones that set off her striking white hair and icy blue eyes. She looked fantastic (it was clear where the Diamond daughters got their good looks) even though she couldn't be bothered to smile. Aunt Phoebe, Kelly's mom, was attending to Grandmother's every need, as usual. And as usual, she was annoying Tamara.

"Can I get you something to eat, Mother?" Phoebe asked, fiddling with her necklace. The creamy pearls were three shades lighter than her dark-blonde hair, and along with her stiff jacket and skirt made her look ultra preppy, and ultra uptight.

"That's what waiters are for, dear." Tamara did not even look at her middle daughter when she answered. Alison tried not to smirk. Aunt Phoebe doted on her mother the same way she doted on her daughter, and Kelly always brushed it off just like Tamara did. But Alison knew that Phoebe was Kelly's rock – even if Kelly would never admit it. It was weird that Kelly had no idea how much she needed her own mother – and loved her, too.

If Kelly were there to witness the scene, she would be making gagging faces behind her mom's back and threatening to trip the waiters with their laden silver trays. She liked to mess with the tuxedoed troops and almost always managed to befriend them and score extra hors d'oeuvres even though she mocked them and called them penguins when they weren't listening. Where was Kelly, anyway?

"So tell me, how's my sister doing?" Aunt Christine slipped her arm through Alison's before she could get away. With her other hand she lifted a champagne flute off a passing tray. "Is she OK?" Her voice dripped with fake concern.

Alison smiled airily and shrugged out of Christine's grasp. "I really should greet the birthday girl," she said, trying to look apologetic.

"Alison!" Grandmother Diamond smiled slightly and held her arms open, waiting for an embrace. The crowd formed a circle around the pair as Alison kissed her grandmother's powdered cheek and let the old woman squeeze the air around her. They were not usually huggers. This was strictly for show.

"Happy birthday, Grandmother," Alison said, forcing a smile. "You look wonderful, as always."

"I don't know what all the fuss is about," Tamara said with a wave of her arm. "At my age, birthdays are a dime a dozen."

Alison kept smiling. "All the fuss" was carefully orchestrated and paid for by Grandma D herself.

Tamara Diamond leaned closer to her granddaughter. Alison thought she was coming in for another hug. But what happened instead was even weirder. "I hope your mother is doing all right," she whispered into Alison's ear. "I am here for *both* of you. You'll let me know if there is anything I can do," she added carefully. It was not a question. It was an offer – a loaded one.

Not sure what to say, Alison just nodded awkwardly. Her grandmother had barely acknowledged that Alison *had* a mother for as long as she could remember. She basically acted like Helen was dead. Alison had expected her family would pry her for info about her mom, but this was a surprisingly bold move on her grandmother's part. Accepting "help" from Tamara Diamond was not always helpful. She kept a tight grip on her purse strings, and careful track of who owed her favours. Alison couldn't even begin to imagine what her grandmother might be hoping to gain from the offer. Thankfully Kelly picked that moment to make an entrance.

"Al, you made it!" Kelly swooped in and broke up the pair, grabbing Alison by the hand. "I wasn't sure you were going to show."

"Kelly, Alison and I were having a conversation," Grandmother Diamond said with a withering glare. Tamara hated interruptions . . . and nicknames.

"Kelly, don't forget your manners," Phoebe hissed at her daughter. She hovered behind Grandmother Diamond, looking embarrassed by Kelly's behaviour. "Alison just got here – I haven't even gotten to say hello yet." Aunt Phoebe forced a smile and reached for Alison as Tamara turned her back to all of them. She did not have time for etiquette lessons or embarrassing family moments. Her public was waiting.

"Say hello." Kelly elbowed Alison, who only had time to give an awkward squeeze to Aunt Phoebe before her cousin pulled her away through the crowd. It was a rude move, for sure. But Kelly was confident she could get away with it. She knew her mother wouldn't dare raise her voice or make a scene in front of Grandmother Diamond and her guests. Phoebe was always fretting about what her mother would think.

Alison gratefully let Kelly lead her past the giant flower arrangements and rooms filled with impeccably dressed guests. She knew they were headed for the pool house. It was their special bungalow. They even slept in there together whenever they spent the night at Grandmother's. It was the perfect place to escape to now.

"Hey – isn't that the skirt I wanted?" Alison stopped in her tracks as Kelly stepped on to the patio. She'd suddenly noticed what her cousin was wearing: the Betsey Johnson skirt Alison had tried on the day before, paired with a tiny tank and loose-knit sweater shrug. She looked amazing.

"Oh, yeah," Kelly answered breezily. "I bought it last night. You can borrow it if you want."

Alison felt stung. Kelly didn't even seem the least bit sorry. But whatever. She was not in the mood to start anything. Right now she was just glad to be out of the party.

Kelly threw open the door to the pool house and stepped inside. "Oh, Al, I hope you don't mind . . . I invited Chad," she said, flopping down on the brightly patterned couch almost on top of Alison's boyfriend.

Alison watched Chad knock Kelly's legs off his lap and stand up. He looked really surprised to see her, and not totally in a good way. "Alison." Chad put his arms around her.

It felt so fabulous to lean against him that Alison ignored the creepy feeling growing in the pit of her stomach. She'd really been missing Chad. She'd almost forgotten how cute he was. They hadn't even had a chance to talk on the phone with all the crazy stuff going on. It was nice of Kelly to think of her and invite him. An afternoon with the two most important people in her life was just what Alison needed.

"Want one?" Behind the bar, Kelly held up a soda. Chad pulled away from Alison and made a mitt with his hands to catch it. Kelly tossed two and Chad opened Alison's. Then the three of them slumped on the couch together.

"So, how's it going? Are you. . . Is your mom. . . I mean, do you know when she's getting out or anything?" Chad looked at Alison quickly, then back at his drink.

This was the part she'd been dreading. The questions. Alison took a gulp of soda. She couldn't even count the times she'd wished her mother would just disappear. But now that she was gone, it was . . . weird. And humiliating. At that moment she didn't want to talk about it – not even with Chad and Kelly.

"Sorry, I, uh, forgot to give Her Highness her present." Alison stood up and smoothed the creases in her trousers. "I'd better go do that."

"Yeah, quick, before she croaks," Kelly joked, scooting over to fill the space next to Chad. She smiled at Alison. "Hurry back."

Chapter 6

The moment Kelly heard the pool door latch, she leaned in so close to Chad she could smell the warm soapy scent of his neck. "See? What did I tell you? She's avoiding you."

Chad nodded slowly and turned to face Kelly. "But I can't break up with her now. She's in trouble . . . I mean, her family is. She needs our help." He paused, his face just inches from Kelly's. "Doesn't she?"

Kelly held her hands up in surrender. "All I know is that she told me she was going to break up with you before all of this happened." Kelly looked down at her new skirt. It looked much better on her than it had on Alison. And so would Chad. She looked back up into Chad's big brown eyes. They were full of questions. And she had the answers. It was kind of amazing how easy it was to lie to him – and how easily he seemed to be buying it.

"If you want to nurse her through this knowing that she's using you, that's your business. But I guarantee she's going to drop you the minute it all blows over . . . just like she was planning to drop you last week. I'm just looking out for you."

Chad looked away. "She just seems so . . . *fragile* right now."

"Are you kidding?" Kelly smirked. "Alison's tough. Like mother, like daughter, right?" Kelly could see him looking at the hair falling across her cheek. She was waiting for him to brush it back behind her ear. She tilted her chin towards him. "But, you know," Kelly lied again, "not everyone in our family is hard as nails."

Chad brushed the hair away from her eyes. A slow smile started at one corner of his mouth.

"That's what I hear," he said.

Chapter 7

"Oh, it's you." Aunt Christine started, nearly upsetting her wine glass as Kelly got into the hot tub. "You scared me."

"Don't be frightened." Kelly gasped a little as she quickly lowered her body into the steaming water. "I won't bite." She knew better. Christine would bite back, and harder.

Kelly looked at her aunt through the steam. It acted like a soft-focus lens, making Christine look as gorgeous as she did on-screen when she was loaded with make-up. *She may be past her prime*, Kelly thought, *but she's undeniably beautiful*. In truth, Kelly looked a lot like her – minus the nips and tucks.

"So, how's our little Alison?" Aunt Christine asked, almost managing to sound like she cared. Definitely not an Oscar-worthy performance. But Kelly was feeling generous. And she was trying to avoid helping her mom do post-party damage control inside.

"She's holding up OK," Kelly said. "For now."

Aunt Christine could not suppress a giggle.

Kelly laughed along with her. Green eyes and blonde

hair were not the only things Kelly and her aunt shared. They both thrived on scandal. Watching it. Living it. Creating it.

Aunt Christine leaned back against the edge of the tub and closed her eyes. "Poor thing," she said. "Do you think she's seen those mother–daughter photos in the tabloids?"

Kelly snorted. "You mean the shots of Aunt Helen and Al in matching yellow Easter dresses?" Alison would just die if she knew. The picture was totally staged and totally lame – one of Helen's "perfect family" moments. "I don't think so. Alison hasn't been out much, and Aunt Helen would never read 'that sort of trash'. Maybe I'll have to pick one up for her."

Christine and Kelly laughed together again, then fell silent. It was moments like these when Kelly almost trusted her youngest aunt. They were the bad girls of the family. The ones who didn't care to put on the perfect act for Tamara. Not that they didn't try to keep on her good side. Nothing was more important than staying on "the list".

"Do you think Aunt Helen's off?" Kelly broke the silence. There was no need to explain off *what* – Aunt Christine always had her mother's money on her mind. Even though Tamara had supposedly taken Helen out of her will years and years ago, there were always rumours that Helen was still included. Nobody but Tamara knew for sure, of course, but after this arrest. . .

"Definitely off the list. Now if we can just get Alison crossed out, too, we'll all be sitting prettier." Aunt Christine did not bother to open her eyes. For a moment Kelly wondered if she was plotting to get *her* taken out of the will, too, or her mother. But for some reason Aunt Christine never seemed to go after Phoebe, and Kelly thought maybe she fell under her mother's umbrella of protection . . . for now.

Slowly Kelly slid under the water until it closed over her head. A funny thought occurred to her as the hot water bubbled around her. Maybe *none* of them were in the will. For all they knew, Her Highness planned to take every last penny with her to the grave. Maybe she was just dangling the promise of inheritance to keep them in her debt . . . and at one another's throats. Tamara simply loved to bring up "the list" at family gatherings and holidays. Her will was a constant source of speculation and feuding. The tabloids had recently declared that Grandmother was worth more than Oprah. But Kelly knew that you couldn't always believe rumours . . . or Aunt Christine.

"What if Aunt Helen gets cleared?" she asked, popping up and letting the water stream down her hair and face.

"Oh, she'll make sure that doesn't happen."

"Really? You think Grandmother will get mixed up in this?"

"Oh, Kelly, don't be naïve." Aunt Christine motioned with her eyes towards the open French doors where

Grandmother Diamond was silhouetted. She stood, barely moving, smugly surveying her pool and back gardens.

"She's already gone beyond stirring the pot." Christine smiled slyly, her voice a whisper. "She cooked this whole thing up. In fact, it's an old family recipe."

Chapter 8

Way too early on Monday morning, Zoey Ramirez followed her twin brother, Tom, into Stafford Academy. She had fallen back to sleep in the car on the way there and had almost missed the winding drive, clipped hedges, and just-as-clipped students gathering on campus. Stafford did not require its students to wear uniforms like they did at her last school, but it may as well have. To Zoey, every kid there looked like they'd got a memo regarding the style du jour and followed it to the letter.

Slinging her messenger bag over her other shoulder, Zoey flipped her long, dark, blonde-streaked bangs out of her face. Zoey hadn't gone to school in Silver Spring since the fifth grade, and she was not particularly happy to be back. She gave the inside of Stafford a once-over and sniffed. The long, clean halls were lined with overflowing trophy cases sending a crystal-clear message: Stafford was for winners.

So what am I doing here? Zoey wondered. School had already been in session for a few weeks. For Zoey it was the first day. She knew she *should* concentrate on fitting in and catching up. But Zoey was not particularly good at doing what she should.

Further down the corridor, trophy cases finally gave way to lockers – the one thing that made tenth grade different from fifth. Students clustered with their kind. Zoey scowled past the jock block and waded through cheerleaders watching Tom make his way down the hall. His confident stride and winning smile reminded Zoey of the way their father, the district attorney, worked the room at schmoozy political events. Ugh. Since when did Tom get so popular?

Before she left for boarding school nearly five years ago, Zoey and her twin had been close. Now she felt like she hardly knew him. Granted, it had only been a few days since she had moved back to Silver Spring, but she and Tom had barely even spoken. He certainly hadn't asked her how she'd liked her most recent boarding school (the last in a long line), or why she was back so soon – or so suddenly. Not that Zoey felt like spilling her guts to him . . . or anybody. But it would have been nice for her brother, at least, to ask for her side of the story.

Zoey followed Tom's back, wondering where he was going and how long she should stick with him. She didn't know if she could hang with his crowd and did *not* want to look like she was leeching. On the other hand, she didn't exactly have anywhere else to go. . .

But the moment Zoey saw where Tom was headed, she

stopped dead in her tracks. Chad Simon was leaning against his locker at the end of the hall. He raised a hand in greeting when he spotted Tom. Chad had been Tom's best friend for ever and was harmless enough. What made Zoey stop was the Bebe-clad snake draped over his shoulder – Kelly Reeves.

What in the world was Chad doing with Kelly? Last Zoey had heard, Chad belonged to Alison Rose. Those cousins shared too much.

The thought of Alison and the sight of Kelly combined to knock the wind right out of Zoey. She staggered back against a locker, hoping nobody would notice the look of pain and disgust on her face. The sting of what Alison and her cousin had done to Zoey back in fifth grade hadn't mellowed a bit, even after all these years. It didn't take much to make Zoey spiral back to that horrible night when Alison had betrayed her – and Zoey's whole world fell apart.

The sleepover was lousy from the get-go ... mother-chaperoned party games, unchaperoned truth or dare, lots of whispering between Alison and Kelly – never with Zoey. There were the usual unexplained giggles. And whispers. But Zoey was never *in on the joke, which could only mean one thing: she* was *the joke.*

Then the phone rang.

"Kelly, sweetie, it's for one of your friends." Phoebe Reeves's

voice crackled over the intercom in the huge family room the six girls had taken over and covered with sleeping bags, magazines and snack foods.

Kelly grabbed the extension. "You rang?" she said rudely. She sounded vaguely annoyed that her party had been interrupted. They'd been talking about boys, and Kelly was just about to tell her anxious followers who her latest lucky crush was so that they could all like him, too.

"For you." Kelly handed the phone to Zoey abruptly. Out of the corner of her eye Zoey saw Alison look at the ceiling. "Next time hire an assistant," Kelly hissed. Zoey's face flamed and she took the cordless into the bathroom and closed the door behind her to shut out the laughter of the other girls.

"Hello?" she said.

"Zoey?" Tom's voice sounded funny, like he had been punched in the stomach. Zoey suddenly felt like she'd been punched, too. "It's Mom," he said.

It was all he had to say. A few minutes later Zoey was changed back into her street clothes and cramming her sleeping bag into its sack.

"So, you're just going to leave?" Kelly asked, incredulous. Nobody left her parties before they were over. Nobody. Ever. Even if they were the butt of the joke. But that was not why Zoey was leaving.

"I have to go," Zoey said quietly. She looked at Alison, who, until that night, she had thought of as her best friend.

She wished she could tell her what was wrong – what was going on. But she couldn't. She could not say it. Not here. Not now.

Alison didn't even meet her gaze. Instead she looked at her cousin and in a mocking tone said, "Zoey has to run home to Mommy!" The other girls cracked up and joined in the taunting.

All Zoey could do was flee in horror. She grabbed her stuff, fighting back tears. They had no idea. And that just made it worse.

Running out of the house, she heard Kelly's mother, Phoebe, call after her. Zoey ignored her and kept running. The gate on the driveway was closed, but it didn't stop her. Zoey heaved her bags over it and climbed up after them.

The sound of a locker slamming right next to her jolted Zoey out of her head. She took a deep breath to clear the memory and stood up straight. She'd thought the party was bad. What had happened after that was a hundred times worse. Zoey had vowed that night that she would never be the fool again.

She tried hard to forget, but would not forgive. In fact, if she had anything to say about it, her former best friend Alison was going to find out what it felt like to have her life destroyed. Zoey hid a wry smile behind her hand. From the look of things around here, Alison's demise had already begun. The news of Helen Rose's arrest was everywhere. It was clear Chad was not stepping up to catch Alison's fall, and Kelly hadn't helped a soul in her life. Alison Rose was standing on the edge of a cliff just waiting for a little push.

Chapter 9

Even in a good week Alison hated Mondays, and this was nowhere close to being a good week. She had prepared herself for the worst. Her earphones were in and she was listening to a playlist she had put together – the soundtrack for a happier life – so she would not have to hear any whispers in the hall. On her feet she wore her favourite red Pumas – the ones her mom hated – so she could run away if she had to. All she needed now was a small army of supporters to get her through the school day. She needed to find her best friend, pronto.

After Grandmother Diamond's party, Alison had gone home feeling strange and confused. Tamara's offer, Chad's distance – and what was with Kelly wearing *her* skirt? – none of it added up. Unable to handle one more prodding comment or pitying look, Alison had slipped some money out of her grandmother's dresser drawer, called a cab, and left early. She'd thought she needed support. Turned out she'd just needed to be alone.

She was home when she saw the magazine on the table in the kitchen. It was one of the rags Elise liked to read that specialized in humiliating celebrities by showing pics of them looking fat or not wearing make-up. It was the kind of trash Helen hated, and normally it wasn't Alison's thing, either. But she was looking for distraction. She'd take what she could get. She picked it up to see what lame-o celeb they were embarrassing this week and choked on her bottled water.

The lame-o was *her*. There she was with her mom, in a full-colour two-page spread. Not just once, three times. The caption below a picture of her and her mom in embarrassing matching outfits read: LIKE MOTHER, LIKE DAUGHTER? Alison suddenly felt dizzy. They were implying she was a criminal!

Alison pushed the horrible night and the horrible magazine from her mind and quickened her pace towards her locker, where she hoped her friends would be waiting. The only way she was going to make it out of this black hole was with the help of Chad and Kelly and the rest of their group. She needed to set things straight with Chad, get to the bottom of the weird vibe she had been feeling at the party, and tell Kelly that if she had really wanted the skirt she should have just said something at the store. It was no big deal.

Spotting the back of Chad's curly head, Alison felt her mouth start to curve up in a smile. He was so cute. And so sweet. Easily the nicest guy at Stafford. As she focused on his curls, she saw something winding its way through them – a hand – playing with the locks, twisting his curls around perfectly manicured fingers with Frostbite-coloured nails. She didn't have to see any more to know who the fingers belonged to. Alison had seen those fingers getting into things they didn't belong in all her life. Kelly was playing with her boyfriend's hair!

"What do you think you're doing?" Alison could hear the quiver in her voice over her music. She did not bother to pull out her earphones. She only wished they could drown out everything that was going on. Kelly's arm was draped over Chad's shoulder, and she didn't look remotely apologetic.

"Here we go," Kelly said to Chad, ignoring Alison. She rolled her eyes and assumed an expression of absolute boredom.

Chad whipped around. He looked surprised and caught. "Alison. Hey," he mumbled. "I didn't think you were coming back to school yet."

"Obviously," Alison choked out. She looked Kelly straight in the face and begged with her eyes for this not to be happening. Not this. Not now.

Kelly flashed a cruel, cold smile. "Welcome back, Al," she cooed. She ran her nails down the back of Chad's neck. "Chad, tell her."

"I've been thinking," Chad said to his shoes.

"It looks like you've been doing more than thinking." Alison found her tongue. It was that thing in her mouth that suddenly seemed as big as a jumbo hot dog.

"Well, um, we were pretty much broken up, anyway," Chad said with a shrug. He looked at Kelly, as if for confirmation, and to continue avoiding Alison's gaze.

Broken up? *Broken up?* "We weren't broken up at all!" Alison said loudly. This *had* to be a joke. Alison looked from Kelly to Chad and back. Everyone else in the hall had gone silent. Alison felt like she was drowning. She wanted to run, but willed herself not to. This couldn't be happening.

"Tell her what you told me, Chad," Kelly purred.

"You haven't really been yourself lately." Chad spoke to the air next to Alison's head. Alison didn't even bother trying to catch his eye. Whatever was going on, it had nothing to do with Chad – and everything to do with Kelly.

Alison stepped closer, so she was just an arm's length away from the two people she used to trust most in the world. "In case you haven't noticed, I have a lot going on in my life," she said hoarsely.

Chad's big brown puppy eyes were full of guilt. "I'm so—" he started, but then Kelly slipped her hand into his.

"You're. . .?" she prompted. Alison wanted to throw up. They had this rehearsed!

"It was over before any of this other stuff happened," he mumbled.

Alison listened to Chad without taking her eyes off her former friend. Kelly met her gaze, unblinking.

The two cousins stared at each other. Kelly, coolly. Alison, fighting back angry tears. It was no surprise that

Kelly could be awful. She had turned on her cousin before with no better reason than boredom. She had done it more times than Alison liked to think about. Kelly wounded for fun. For sport. But this was a whole new level of cruel, even for Kelly. Even for a Diamond.

Finally Alison blinked. With music still wailing in her ears, she turned and walked off in silence.

Chapter 10

Walk, Alison told herself. *Take a step*. She forced herself to put one foot in front of the other slowly in spite of a burning desire to run as fast as she could. She could hear Kelly's shrill laughter echoing off the cement walls. She could feel everyone's eyes on her back. She raised her head and squared her shoulders. If her mother had taught her anything, it was how to put up a facade. Nobody had to know she was broken inside.

Turning a corner, Alison stumbled up the stairs to the second floor. She wanted to dissolve into a puddle of tears right then and there. But she had to make it to some kind of haven, somewhere at least a little bit safe before breaking down. Alison blinked and realized that her vision was blurring. A couple of students stared as she walked past. Just some chattering freshmen, thank goodness. Up ahead she could see the girls' loo. Not perfect, but good enough.

Alison pushed open the door, holding her breath. The loos were empty. Rushing into a stall, she locked the door. Before she could even slump down on the toilet, a loud sob escaped her throat and the tears started pouring.

Wrapping her arms around herself, Alison rocked back and forth. *Breathe*, she told herself. If she could just keep breathing she might survive this nightmare.

"Ugh," Alison moaned between sobs. How could Kelly do this to her? *Why* was Kelly doing this to her? What had Alison ever done to Kelly? Alison's despair turned quickly to rage. She wanted to scream. She wanted to break Chad's kneecaps. She wanted to poke Kelly's eyes out. She wanted to. . .

Just then the door to the loos banged open. Alison quickly lifted her feet off the ground and hugged her knees, balancing on the toilet seat. She peered through the crack in the stall but couldn't tell who was on the other side. The girl turned on the tap and splashed some water on her face.

Good idea, Alison thought grimly. She silently pulled out her compact mirror and checked her reflection. She looked pretty bad. Terrible, actually. But thanks to years of living with Helen Rose, she had ways to deal with that – if she ever made it out of the stall. A splash of ice-cold water would be a good first step.

Alison waited while the girl dried her hands and face, checked her hair and make-up in the mirror, and untucked her shirt. *Come on, come on*, she thought. If she was going to make herself look decent before class she had to get going.

Finally Alison heard the door open. The girl was leaving. When the door closed again she stood up, pulled back the latch, and stepped out of the stall. . .

Right in front of Zoey Ramirez. Zoey Ramirez, her old best friend. A shocker, but not a bad one. Alison hadn't seen Zoey since fifth grade. But right at this moment she was in desperate need of a best friend.

"Zoey!" Alison said, smiling widely. "Wow!" The light in the toilets was kind of sketchy – maybe Zoey wouldn't notice that she looked—

"Alison?" Zoey peered at her old friend. "You look horrendous."

That was Zoey. She always called it like she saw it. There was no use lying to her, but that didn't mean Alison had to tell her the whole truth, either. "It's been a rough morning," she admitted. "But I'm all right now."

Zoey raised an eyebrow. "Yeah, I heard about your mom," she said. "And I saw the scene with Kelly and Chad."

Alison stepped up to the mirror. Time to get busy. "Kelly and Chad deserve each other," she said as she turned on the tap full blast. "I can't believe you're back here! How was boarding school?" She splashed her face, then looked up at Zoey's reflection in the mirror. "Tell me. I want to hear everything!"

Chapter 11

Kelly led Chad to her table by the window in the lunchroom and set her tray down with a little swing of her long blonde hair. Smiling sideways at her new and totally hot boyfriend, she slid into her seat. It had only been two days since the scene with Alison in the hall, but everyone knew she had bested the girl. Kelly was loving the attention she and Chad were getting. It even gave her kind of an appetite. But she had opted for the usual – a salad and a bottle of Evian.

"Oooh, I forgot a napkin." Kelly batted her eyelashes at Chad. "Could you go get me one?"

Chad was about to stand up when his best friend, Tom, plunked his tray down across from them. "Here, you can have mine," he offered.

Chad turned and smirked at Tom across the table. "Did you catch the game last night?" he asked.

Tom groaned. "Don't remind me. It was brutal. We should have just forfeited at the half."

Chad snorted unattractively, and Kelly shuddered. Sometimes guys were such . . . *guys*. Not to mention dense.

What was more important, her needing to wipe her chin or a stupid football game?

"Chad," Kelly said, sounding exactly like Her Highness, "that's such an ugly sound."

"Sorry," Chad grumbled as he scooped up a forkful of macaroni cheese.

Bored with the boys, Kelly turned her attention to the rest of the lunchroom. It was a large, airy hall filled with round tables of different sizes, each with its own hanging lamp and live plant to keep it from looking too institutional. The kitchen and large selection of foods – everything from vegan entrées to South Beach fare – was set up along the wall across from the floor-to-ceiling windows behind Kelly. The crowd was segregated into the usual tables of geeks and freaks and brains and jocks. And then there was the table in the corner to which Alison had been exiled.

Since Kelly had humiliated her in the hall on Monday, nobody had been spending much time with – or even talking to – Alison Rose. They were all talking *about* her, though – gossiping about her mother's indictment and speculating on how long Chad and Kelly had been seeing each other behind Alison's back. Kelly felt a little shiver of victorious excitement. She'd known that bringing her cousin down would be easy, but she hadn't realized it would be quite so much fun.

There was only one little fly in her otherwise perfect ointment: Zoey Ramirez. Kelly glared at the girl as she took a seat by Alison. She had heard that Tom's twin was returning to Stafford after a four-year stint at five different boarding schools, and she'd seen for herself what a weirdo Zoey had become. But she'd had no idea that Zoey and Alison would pick up where they'd left off before Kelly'd had to break up their little friendship. How pathetic.

Watching Alison and Zoey with their heads together over their lunch trays, Kelly felt a stab of annoyance. Alison looked . . . fine. She was actually smiling! Had she completely forgotten that her life was *ruined*?

Kelly jabbed a cherry tomato with her fork. For a moment, she was tempted to go over and congratulate Alison on her acting. It had to be acting, didn't it? Alison couldn't possibly have shaken off being humiliated in front of the whole school, and losing her guy *and* Kelly's friendship so easily. Not to mention the fact that her mother was a criminal. Alison just didn't have it in her.

Kelly shoved the tomato into her mouth and exploded it to bits between her molars. Time to take things up a notch – a big notch. She looked across the table at Zoey's twin, who was obliviously munching on a carrot. Kelly had always liked Tom well enough – he was cute and funny and had never got in her way. And now he might even come in handy.

Kelly took a sip of spring water and leaned across the table towards Tom. She smiled up at him. "Zoey seems to be doing great," she said sweetly. "I'm sure she's thrilled to be back."

Tom coughed on his carrot stick. "Not exactly," he admitted.

Kelly leaned in closer and put her hand on his forearm. "Really?" she asked innocently.

Tom nodded and his cheeks reddened slightly. Kelly had him under her spell. "Yeah, she had no choice. She's been kicked out of five schools in a row. And after what she did at her last school, Dad really had to pull some strings to get her into Stafford."

Bingo. "Oh, I'm sure she didn't do anything too terrible," Kelly cooed. "Boarding schools can be so uptight."

"I have no idea what she did," Tom admitted. "But whatever it was got her kicked out hard and fast. If she pulls any stunts here. . ." He trailed off, a concerned look crossing his broad, tanned face. Kelly knew what he was thinking. He was hoping that Zoey would not drag him down now that they were in the same school.

Kicked out . . . the words danced around in Kelly's head like blinking lights on a Christmas tree. She turned to look back at Zoey and Alison and smirked. This was just too good. Twirling a lock of hair between her fingers, she contemplated how she was going to use this new ammunition. She was lost in thought when Alison picked up her tray and got to her feet.

Kelly was on her own Miu Miu–clad feet in a second. "Be right back," she said, flashing a smile and giving Chad's shoulder a squeeze. As she stepped away from the table, she had no idea what she was going to say to Alison, but she knew it would come to her. When you were as good as she was, you didn't have to think things all the way through. Timing her walk just so, she met her cousin at the tray drop.

"Hi, Alison!" she said, as if they were still the best of friends. "How is everything?"

Alison's blue eyes flashed as she set her tray on the stainless-steel counter, saying nothing. Then she smiled brightly and turned to face her former friend. "Everything is fine, Kelly," she said. "It's amazing how much better life gets when you get rid of the parasites."

Kelly felt her jaw tighten but smiled sweetly. "Really, Alison," she chided. "You shouldn't talk about your mother that way. The poor woman is in prison!"

"I wasn't referring to my mother," Alison said evenly.

Kelly acted as though she hadn't heard her. "Speaking of Auntie Helen, I wanted to tell you I think it's just horrible who's responsible for her situation. I was shocked when I found out who turned her in. You must be furious."

Finally Alison flinched. "What are you talking about?" she asked quietly.

Kelly savoured the moment – and the expression on Alison's face. "Oh, you don't know?" Kelly asked with a dazzling smile. She waited exactly five more seconds, then leaned forward conspiratorially and spoke just three more words: "Her Royal Highness."

Chapter 12

Chad closed his locker with a slam and spun around. Life was good. Aside from the nagging guilt he had about ditching Alison, he was flying high. Kelly Reeves was most definitely the hottest and richest girl at school – a fine catch for anybody, but especially Chad, who needed to stay on top. It wasn't easy to keep his background and free ride under wraps, but with Kelly as his girlfriend, nobody would question him. Of course, the same could be said of dating Alison. But Alison wasn't as powerful as Kelly. Kelly really knew how to work the system. Any system.

Chad looked around the crowded hallway for Kelly but didn't see her. She seemed to come and go like the tide. That was OK with him. He liked his freedom, or what was left of it. Slinging his pack over his shoulder, Chad headed off to class. Mr Beekler hated it when his students were late.

"Did you see Kelly's new jeans?" he heard a girl say as he made his way through the crowd. "Definitely Sevens."

Designer jeans for a designer girlfriend, Chad thought. He suddenly wondered how he was going to afford her.

Kelly was always buying stuff, always eating out. She would probably expect Chad to start coming along and laying down cash. Alison wasn't so much of a spender, he realized. That was one good thing about her.

Actually, there were lots of good things about Alison. She was smart, beautiful, funny, sweet. . . He still couldn't believe that she'd burned him. He'd had no idea that she was planning to dump him. He hadn't even believed it when Kelly first told him. But Kelly insisted it was true, and then Alison didn't call him when her mom got arrested . . . or take his call the next day. And she acted so weird at the party – what was up with that? Chad had been waiting to comfort her, but she'd barely said hello to him before taking off. He'd felt totally stupid.

Chad shook his head as he rounded a corner. He had to get over it. He was with Kelly. And whether he still cared about her or not, Alison was like poison now. She'd been exiled. Best to stop thinking about her completely.

Checking the clock on his mobile, Chad looked up just in time to stop himself from walking right into the very person he'd just vowed to avoid – Alison. His shoes squeaked to a halt on the tile floor.

"Hey," he said, trying to sound casual. Inside he was freaking. This was so awkward. He hoped nobody would see them together.

"Hey," Alison said, looking up at him with her big blue eyes. She looked like she'd been crying, or trying really hard not to. And her voice was soft, vulnerable. He'd never heard her like that before.

Chad's heart thudded in his chest. He had to stop himself from putting his arms around her. For some reason, hugging her seemed like the thing to do. The thing he *wanted* to do. Only he couldn't, of course. He shouldn't even be talking to her. But he couldn't just stand there. . .

Chad looked around. They were basically alone. "Listen, I'm really sorry about—"

"There you are, Chad," Kelly said smoothly as she glided up to them out of nowhere. Chad immediately stiffened and took a step back from Alison. He didn't want to make Kelly mad. A ticked-off Kelly was a scary thing. But if she was upset she didn't show it.

"I see you're doing your charity work again," she drawled. "But I'm afraid this cause is hopeless." Without even looking at Alison, she took Chad by the arm and led him away. "Meet me out front after class," she ordered. "My aunt Christine is taking me shopping – we'll give you a ride home."

In a split second the knot of feelings he'd been having over Alison was forgotten. Chad smiled. Kelly's aunt Christine was gorgeous and famous, and everybody knew it. Kelly was offering more than a ride. She was offering a chance to look good in front of everyone at Stafford.

"Sweet," Chad agreed as Kelly gave his hand a little squeeze. He knew Alison was still standing in the hall, but he didn't give his ex-girlfriend a second glance.

Chapter 13

Tom plopped down on the marble steps in front of the school to wait for Chad. They hung out at Tom's place together most days after school . . . or used to. These days Kelly frequently had something she wanted Chad to do – a lot more than Alison used to. Chad never complained, though – and why should he? Dating Kelly was cool; Tom knew that.

"Hey, Tom," Kelly said, coming up behind him. "Could you hold this for a sec?" She handed him her Balenciaga metallic tote before he could reply. "Thanks, you're a sweetie."

Tom blushed. "No problem," he said. "I love a fashionable accessory."

Kelly laughed. *Mission accomplished*, Tom thought. If you can't have the girl of your dreams, at least you can impress her with your dorky sense of humour.

Tom watched as Kelly pulled her MAC compact out of her purse and put on some lip gloss. It was a pretty pink shade – not too obvious. The perfect choice, of course.

"Have you seen Chad?" Kelly asked, slipping the gloss and the compact back into her purse.

"Unh-uh."

Kelly's gorgeous green eyes narrowed as she scanned the lawn. "I told him to meet me here right after class." She sounded annoyed.

Tom nodded. "I'm sure he'll be here any second," he said. "He's not stupid enough to stand up a beautiful blonde."

Just then Aunt Christine pulled up to the kerb and honked her horn. A bunch of students turned to gawk at the actress in her sporty Mercedes. Kelly waved. "Be right there!" she shouted.

"Where is he?" she asked, sounding thoroughly put out. "Aunt Christine doesn't like to be kept waiting."

And neither do you, Tom thought. But then, why should a girl like Kelly have to wait for anything? If she were his, he'd never keep her—

"What's up?" greeted a voice behind them.

"Your number," Tom mumbled to himself. "You almost missed your ride, man," he said more loudly, nodding towards Aunt Christine. She was checking herself out in the flip-down mirror, pretending not to notice she was drawing a crowd.

"Where have you been?" Kelly asked, lacing her fingers through Chad's and giving him a pout. "You were supposed to be here ten minutes ago."

"Sorry," Chad said. "Mrs Naslund kept me after class."

"Next time tell her you have an appointment with Hollywood," Tom said.

Kelly smiled. "Right," she agreed with a laugh. She gave Chad's hand a little tug. "Come on, let's go. You want a ride, Tom?"

Tom glanced up at Kelly's green eyes. He wanted to come. And he didn't. He'd had a crush on Kelly since grade school, and this had been the year he was going to get her. Until she set her sights on his best friend, Chad.

"No, thanks," he said. "I'll just walk."

"OK," Kelly said, obviously not giving it a second thought as she pulled Chad towards the waiting car.

Tom watched them go. He ignored the stabbing feeling in his heart as best he could.

Half an hour later Tom unlocked the door to his house and stepped inside the cool entry hall. He hadn't even closed the door when he heard voices – two of them. Zoey was hanging out with someone.

Kicking off his shoes, a habit picked up when Debbie 2 (the second in a long line of narrowly avoided stepmother candidates) was in power a couple of years ago, Tom followed the voices into the kitchen. His sister and Alison Rose were sitting across from each other at the counter, laughing. The sound was foreign. It didn't really go with the house, and it took a second for Tom to realize why. Zoey never laughed any more. So why was she laughing with Alison? Had she forgotten what her "best friend" did to her back in fifth grade?

"What's up?" Tom asked, giving Alison a little wave. If they had been at school, he wouldn't even have made eye contact – being nice to Alison had become social suicide. But Tom couldn't exactly ignore her when she was sitting right there in his kitchen. Besides, she looked kind of cute with her hair pulled back in low ponytails. Good looks ran in the family.

"Not much," Zoey replied. It was probably the longest conversation they'd had since Zoey's latest expulsion. Tom found it hard to believe they were even related, let alone that they had once been totally tight. Oh, well. His sister's return to Silver Spring hadn't exactly made Tom's life easier. Their dad was so worked up over whatever it was Zoey had done that now *both* of them were under extra-intense scrutiny. Thanks to Zoey, Tom was under even more pressure than normal never to screw up.

Tom opened the cupboard and pulled out a giant bowl and a box of Cap'n Crunch. "Want some?" he offered as he began to pour.

Alison shook her head and smiled. "Some things never change," she said.

Tom topped off the bowl. "More for me," he said as he added some milk. He was spooning up the sweet crunchies before he had even put the milk away. He and the Cap'n went way back. Sugary cereal was the thing that got him through elementary school.

"Remember the time we put shredded wheat in the Crunch Berries box?" Alison said, her eyes bright.

Zoey laughed. "Oh, man. That was perfect." She eyed her munching brother. "When you realized what was in your bowl you looked like someone ran over your dog."

"It wasn't funny," Tom said gravely, remembering the prank. It had actually been a little devastating. "But that was a long time ago. Forgive and forget, right?" he said pointedly, looking right at Zoey. He had no idea what was up between these girls, but he hoped it was all cool. For both of them.

Just then the front door slammed and their district attorney dad walked into the kitchen, talking loudly on his mobile phone.

"I need it done today," he bellowed, waving his hand wildly. "No excuses."

"How was your day, kids?" Tom whispered to the girls with a roll of his eyes. His dad couldn't care less about his own kids, and it burned Tom up.

"Great, Dad, how about yours?" Zoey answered quietly. Not that it mattered. Mr Ramirez was talking so loudly he wouldn't have heard them if they shouted.

"All right, fine. Call me when it's done." Mr Ramirez flipped his phone closed and stood in the kitchen with a smug expression on his chiselled face. "I have great news," he said, clearly bursting to tell someone. He looked at the three kids sitting in front of him, then past them in search of somebody better to tell. There was nobody there, of course. "Do you know who you're looking at?" He held his arms wide and waited for an answer.

A lousy dad, a jerk, a slimeball? Tom thought. Any of those would be accurate.

"Our next congressional candidate!" he blurted.

Tom stared at his father. "You're running for Congress?" he asked incredulously. "Don't you have to be an honest person to do that?" he added. He regretted it immediately.

"What is that crack supposed to mean?" his father shot back. "I suggest you focus on yourself and start growing up, Cap'n." He knocked the cereal box with his knuckle and stepped closer to his son. His voice got deeper and quieter as he spoke. Not a good sign. "When you are making straight As, playing first string, and getting scholarship offers from Ivy League colleges, you might be able to offer me advice. But not before."

Tom felt a flash of annoyance. His dad was always on him to do more, do better. As it was, Tom was no slouch. But no matter what he did, it wasn't enough. Besides, what about Zoey?

"Why are you lecturing *me*?" Tom asked hotly. *You're no great example, and—* "I'm not the one who got kicked out of boarding school." He lobbed the ball of flame into his sister's court.

Across the table, Zoey glared.

Chapter 14

Whoa. Alison looked from Zoey to Tom and back to Zoey, who looked ready to explode. Not that she could blame her. That was a low blow. Alison hadn't realized Tom was capable of being anything other than nice and funny. And she'd never seen a family fight as dirty as hers did. The Ramirez clan was coming pretty close.

"Zoey is another matter," Mr Ramirez said in his deep, rumbling growl. He sounded like a tiger coiled to pounce. "For another time," he added, eyeballing his daughter. Then he levelled his smouldering gaze at Tom, giving him one last angry look before he turned his back on the kids and left the room.

"Whoa!" Alison said, breaking the icy silence the DA left in his wake. "Well, he's as friendly as ever."

"As ever," Zoey repeated, rolling her eyes. They laughed, and the tension melted. "What were we talking about? Cap'n Crunch?"

Alison grinned. She loved the way Zoey could shake things off and move on. Like, she obviously wasn't holding a grudge about that awful night in fifth grade. And just now her brother had totally messed with her and, as far as Alison could tell, Zoey wasn't kicking him under the counter or anything. Watching her new/old best friend play with a few pieces of cereal, Alison wondered why she had turned on her in the first place . . . even though she knew the answer.

Kelly. The name swam around in her brain like a great white shark. Kelly was the one who hadn't liked Zoey. Probably felt threatened by her, Alison realized. And Alison had been stupid enough to let Kelly goad her into humiliating Zoey in the worst way – on what turned out to be the worst possible night.

Tom dumped the last of the cereal into his bowl and added more milk. "It's always a little sad when there are only a few bites left." He shook his head and clutched his chest.

Alison smiled. Tom was cute – something she'd never really noticed before. Probably because she had been too focused on Chad. But that was no longer an issue . . . even though she sort of wished it were. Chad had been a good boyfriend – funny, handsome, clever. Alison still couldn't believe he had ditched her for Kelly. Didn't he realize Kelly was just using him? He couldn't really be falling for her. Could he?

Alison sighed. Who was she kidding? Her cousin was beautiful, popular, crazy and fun. Everyone fell for Kelly. Including her.

The front door opened again and Debbie 5 (actually

named Deirdre) stepped into the house. She strolled into the kitchen and dumped her hideous and huge last-season Gucci bag on the counter.

Alison blinked at the woman standing before her. She wore a tight-fitting dress with a wide belt and a ridiculously low neckline. It was hard not to stare at her obviously surgically enhanced figure. She looked like a Barbie.

"Did you hear?" she squealed excitedly. "Your dad is running for Congress! Congress of the *United States*!" She spun around as if in a dream.

"Really?" Zoey said with exaggerated interest. "Of the United States? Gosh, I figured he'd be running in Mexico or Guam."

Deirdre ignored the smart-aleck remark. "Imagine me, a congressman's wife!"

Alison coughed and covered her mouth with her hand, trying not to laugh out loud. Tom's face, on the other hand, suddenly shifted into a mask of annoyance.

"Yes, we heard," he said.

"Well, where *is* that future politician?" Deirdre asked, her hazel eyes wide.

"On the phone," Zoey said, jerking her thumb towards the den. "I think the pope called, or something."

"The pope!" Deirdre screamed.

Tom snorted, and Deirdre's face fell. "Oh, that was a joke, right?"

Zoey rolled her eyes. "Um, right."

Deirdre left the kitchen with a clatter of high heels on tile. The smell of her perfume stayed behind.

"Ugh," Zoey grumbled, fanning the air in front of her nose. "I think she's the worst Debbie yet."

"Definitely," Tom agreed. "If only her brain were as big as her. . ."

"Bag," Zoey finished with a sly grin.

"I'd take Debbie number two over her any day," Tom announced, dumping his bowl in the sink. "Her rules were weird, but at least she had a brain."

Zoey nodded her agreement as she picked up the TV remote and hit a button.

Alison sucked in her breath. The news was on. And Helen Rose was the lead story.

Chapter 15

Zoey could not believe her luck. She stared at the image of the perfectly styled woman on the television screen. Her face looked composed in spite of the fact that she was surrounded by throngs of shouting reporters and a pack of lawyers leading her into the county courthouse. Zoey had seen Helen Rose before, of course, but had forgotten just how poised she was. On-screen she almost looked . . . fake. Not human.

"Change the channel, Zoey," Tom hissed, looking sideways at Alison, who was staring at the screen as if she'd seen a ghost. Zoey tightened her fingers around the remote sitting on the counter but didn't turn the television off. This was too sweet an opportunity to let slide. Alison had followed her home after school like a puppy for three days straight, and Zoey was getting a little bored. It was time to get her revenge plan rolling.

"It's not like this is news to Alison," Zoey said easily as she watched Alison's reaction. "You've seen it all before, right?" she asked with a smile. The tidbit on the news was a welcome surprise. A chance to see Alison squirm. . .

But if Alison was shaken, she didn't let it show. Like mother, like daughter. "Right," she said woodenly. "Old news."

Zoey hit the volume button, and the sound of a reporter's voice echoed in the room. "Rose is being held while the police and federal agencies conduct their investigation. As of this evening, no business associates or family members have been cleared of involvement in this unusual financial scandal. But a spokesman from the district attorney's office assures reporters it will be a miracle if anyone comes out of this investigation 'smelling like a Rose'." The reporters laughed. Zoey fought back her own chuckle. This was better than anything she could have planned.

Alison put her hand around the edge of the kitchen counter to steady herself, and Zoey grinned. Alison was already so vulnerable. Revenge was going to be easy . . . and sweet.

Distracted by her plans for payback, Zoey didn't notice Tom getting to his feet. By the time she realized what he was doing, the television was already turned off.

"I think we've seen enough of that," he said, shooting his sister a "what is wrong with you?" look.

Alison nodded as she pushed her stool in and carried her glass to the sink. "I'd better get going," she said, sounding kind of hollow.

"Right," Zoey agreed without getting up. "Catch you tomorrow?"

Alison grabbed her bag off the counter and slung it over her shoulder. "I guess," she said softly. She turned and left the kitchen, making her way through the living room on the way to the door. As Alison passed a shelf full of crystal collectibles, Zoey saw her pick up a small glass elephant figurine and slip it into her pocket.

Zoey had all but forgotten about Alison's little habit. She considered busting her on it but decided not to. She couldn't care less about the trinket – probably left by some Debbie – and if Zoey was going to repay Alison in full, she needed her trust.

As soon as the front door closed, Tom turned to Zoey.

Here we go, Zoey thought. *A lecture from Mister Good Guy*. But before Tom could say anything, a voice called out from the den.

"Zoey, I need to see you for a minute," DA Dad announced. Zoey blew her hair out of her eyes as she strolled casually into the den. What now?

Sitting behind his giant mahogany desk, her dad looked kind of . . . small. Zoey was appreciating that little fact when he opened his mouth and told her another fact that she didn't appreciate at all.

"I've hired a tutor for you," he said flatly, eyeing her over the top of his half-rim reading glasses. Zoey started to protest. He raised his hand to stop her.

"Objection overruled," he said before she'd said a word. "You will see a tutor twice a week until further notice. I will not allow my daughter's delinquency to destroy my reputation. The media would have a field day if they knew what you did. I'm running for Congress – so you'd better shape up."

Zoey's eyes narrowed as she watched her father flip through some papers on his desk. *I'd like to shape* you *up*, Zoey thought. But she knew there was no use in arguing. Her father was a criminal prosecutor who never lost. Ever. And he had just handed down his verdict. Case closed.

Chapter 16

Chad flipped open his geometry textbook. He stared at the figures and tried to ignore the sounds of his shouting parents downstairs. They were going at it . . . again. It seemed like all they did was fight.

As he turned the page and tried to focus, a folded piece of pink paper slipped into his lap. Unfolding it, Chad got a whiff of Kelly's perfume and smiled. She smelled almost as good as she looked.

Chad,
Hope you're having a great night. I miss you!
xoxoxoxo,
Kelly
PS Wear your red collared shirt tomorrow. It's so cute on you.

Chad's heart raced. He wondered if his red shirt – a gift from Alison, actually – was clean. He hated the word *cute*, but somehow when Kelly used it he didn't mind. Chad refolded the paper, tossed it on to his desk, and wondered when

Kelly had slipped it into his book. Between classes? In the car? There hadn't been much time on the ride home, since Kelly spent most of it arguing with her aunt. And then Chad had asked to be dropped off at the mall because he "forgot" something. What he forgot was that if Kelly got an eyeful of where he actually lived she'd drop him off permanently. What had he been thinking? He couldn't get a ride home from Christine. Ever.

Chad shuddered, considering the fallout he'd narrowly avoided. He had to be careful not to let his guard down. Kelly was not like Alison. She would ditch him in a second if she found out he wasn't rich.

A loud knock interrupted Chad's thoughts and made him jump. A slightly darker, just as curly head appeared in the door frame. Then all of Dustin slouched in – unshaven, as usual, and looking kind of wired. "Hey, little bro'," he said, scanning the top of Chad's dresser. Chad sniffed. Dustin was looking for money. And he'd come to the wrong place.

"Hey, Dustin," Chad replied without getting up. "What's up?"

"I was wondering if I could borrow a little cash," Dustin said, his eyes darting across every flat surface he could find. Chad had stopped leaving money lying around his room ages ago – Dustin had a habit of "finding" it and making it disappear. He was always getting mixed up in money-making schemes that were always a little suspect and always total failures.

Chad shook his head. "I'm broke," he fibbed. It was true enough – or would be soon. Dating Kelly Reeves could drain a millionaire's bank account – let alone Chad's meagre savings from his summer job. His allowance had all but dried up since his little brother, Will, had started at an expensive school for autistic kids. The school was supposed to take the pressure off his parents, but it had made money extra tight and, judging from the screaming match still going on downstairs, the pressure was *on*.

"Come on." Dustin fidgeted, shoving his hands in his pockets. "I need forty bucks. I've been playing pool with the guys. I just know I'm going to win next time. Then I can pay off—"

Chad looked up at his brother's pleading eyes. Gambling was not new to his repertoire. But he always ended up losing more than he made. Why didn't he learn? Chad had managed to get a scholarship to a good school and was making it. Didn't Dustin want the same thing?

"Sorry – ask Mom and Dad," Chad said, feeling a little guilty. They were brothers, after all. They were stuck in their disaster of a family together. But he needed every penny to keep things on track with Kelly. And he needed Kelly to keep things on track at school.

Dustin glared at his brother and stepped up to his dresser for a better look. "All right. Ten bucks."

"I don't have it," Chad said, starting to get annoyed. What part of "no" didn't his brother understand? He got to his feet as a new chorus of parental fighting echoed through the open door. Somewhere downstairs Will was hearing all of this.

"I'm gonna check on Will," Chad said, moving towards the door and forcing Dustin to make his way there as well. If he left Dustin in his room, he'd probably ransack the place looking for loose change.

Out in the hall, Chad pulled his door closed. Dustin shuffled back to his own room and when he had closed himself inside, Chad went downstairs.

He knew right where to find Will. He opened the cleaning closet and waited for his eyes to adjust to the dim light. Sitting on the floor, folded up next to the vacuum cleaner with his arms wrapped around his knees, Will was rocking. He rocked back and forth and sang very quietly to himself. Chad figured he sang to block out the noise. But it obviously didn't work, because the poor kid could recite every bitter word their parents said to each other. You never knew when it would happen. Like last night at dinner when Dustin asked Will to pass the peas.

"Do I have to do everything around here?" Will had snarled in perfect imitation of their mom. If it weren't so sad, it would have been funny.

"Hey, buddy." Chad squatted down and tousled Will's soft, brown hair. Now that he was eleven he was not that much shorter than Chad. But he was still a little kid on the inside. "You OK?" Chad asked.

Will looked like he was nodding, but it could have just been the rocking. His body never stopped moving.

"You remember why Mom and Dad fight?" Chad asked.

"They're working it out," Will recited. "Working it out."

"That's right." Chad fished for a tissue in his pocket but didn't come up with it fast enough. Will wiped his nose on Chad's sleeve.

"You up for a hot dog?" Chad asked, speaking softly and raising his eyebrows. Dinner was probably not going to happen any time soon and, when it did, it wasn't going to be pretty. Better to get Will out of the house so he'd have a chance to sleep tonight. The fighting gave him nightmares.

"With relish?" Will finally stopped rocking. His hand found its way into Chad's.

"And extra sauerkraut." Chad smiled. There was a place just three blocks away. They had been going there so often lately it was like home away from home. A little oasis of peace and sustenance – if you considered a processed meat stick sustenance. Anyway, it was what they needed.

Chad checked his wallet – enough for two dogs, two sodas, and a shared fries. This little venture was going to clean him out and burn his study time. After hot dogs Will always wanted Chad to stay with him until he was asleep. Chad would read to him and usually fall asleep himself. It was their routine. With a sigh, Chad realized he would have to call his go-to guy for the answers to his homework again. Sure, it was cheating. And he'd owe his best friend yet another favour. But what choice did he have? He had to take care of Will. He had to keep his grades up. He had to keep it all together.

Thank God for Tom, Chad thought. He could totally trust him, which was essential. If the school ever found out just how much "help" Chad needed, he could kiss his scholarship – and Kelly, and basically his whole life – goodbye.

After quickly writing a note on the dry-erase board on the fridge, Chad started out of the kitchen. His parents had moved the fight to the basement and he did not want to interrupt. For a second, Chad wondered if they knew their underground yelling carried up through the heating vents to every room of the house. They were not sparing anyone; they were broadcasting. He thought about telling them, then thought again. He led Will towards the front door. They had to get out before Will started rocking again.

The two brothers were still holding hands when they reached the sidewalk, and Will pulled Chad to a stop. He looked Chad square in the face – something he didn't do much. "Will they be done fighting when we get back?" he asked.

Chad swallowed. He hated lying to Will. Will didn't get lies. People thought autistic kids were stupid, but they weren't. They knew lots more than people gave them credit for. They weren't dumb; they were sort of . . . pure. They did not get embarrassed. They loved unconditionally. They did not lie, and they did not understand people who did.

A long time ago Chad had pledged never to lie to Will. Never to hurt him. Hard as it was, he could not start now. "Maybe," was all he could say.

Chapter 17

Oh my gosh. Oh my gosh. Oh my gosh. Alison repeated the phrase over and over in her head as the not-just-one-or-two but *three* sets of locking gates and heavy doors opened and then shut again behind her. Each time she heard a lock slide back into place with the cold click of metal on metal she cringed. She'd thought she could handle this. Now she was not so sure.

Beside Alison, one of her mother's attorneys was unflinching. She didn't even bother to hang up her phone, treating the jail hall like a private phone booth. She barely noticed Alison was with her. Alison was secretly grateful her father had an "urgent meeting" that kept him from coming along – even if the meeting probably did take place at a bar.

Emerging into the waiting room, Alison was surprised to see that the jail visiting area looked a lot like the ones on TV. It made it seem familiar. There were chairs lined up facing one another on either side of a centre console. It looked like a long desk separated down the middle and on either side by thick glass. Phones hung in the bulletproof cubicles.

She's not going to be wearing make-up, Alison thought

suddenly. That would be weird. She could not remember the last time she had seen her mother without make-up. Helen would probably give anything for a lipstick. The thought made Alison relax just a little.

A large guard at the door on the prisoner's side announced a new prisoner by number. He unlocked the door and a small, auburn-haired woman walked through. This was not your typical Helen Rose entrance. But she held her head high and smiled when she saw Alison . . . or maybe when she saw her lawyer.

Alison was glad that the lawyer was going to talk first. It gave her a chance to get ready. Standing in the back of the room, she studied her mom. The orange jumpsuit was not doing anything for her. She looked oddly younger and smaller without make-up or heels. And yet she looked older, too.

A lump rose in Alison's throat. This was all wrong. Her mother did not belong here. She belonged on a lawn sipping a citrus cooler, on a yacht wearing an enormous sun hat, on her mobile ordering people around, at home driving Alison crazy. The lump in her throat grew, threatening to choke off her air completely – but not because her mother was suffering injustice. Because, Alison realized, she did not want her mom to get out and come home. At least not any time soon.

The meeting was over quickly. The lawyer stood and waved Alison over. Alison crossed the room in what felt like slow motion. She could see her mom taking in every detail of Alison's appearance. Alison had worked hard to get them right. French manicure (home job since Alison had no cash). Low heels. Gloss with just a hint of colour. *Why am I trying to impress a jailbird?* Alison asked herself. It made her lift her chin a little higher.

"Hi," Alison spoke softly into the phone.

"Hi," Helen replied.

If this were a movie, it would be the part where the reunited mother and daughter pressed their hands together on the glass and let the tears flow. Luckily it was not a movie. All eyes were dry.

"Alison, I know this has been a hard time for you." Helen looked almost concerned as she said it. Alison was caught off guard. Did her mother know about Kelly and Chad? "But I need your help," she finished.

No. This was something else. Something bigger. Alison was silent as her mother leaned closer to the glass. She was serious. Helen Rose was about to ask Alison to do more than play the happy daughter.

"Your Grandmother Diamond set me up," Helen said matter-of-factly. "She is responsible for all of this."

Even though Kelly had said the same thing, Alison hadn't believed it until now. It seemed too much, even for her family. Why would Tamara Diamond want her daughter to be in prison? Wasn't it enough to cut Helen off from the family and take her out of the will? Why would Tamara want to humiliate and destroy her, too?

"Listen to me, Alison. I need your help." Her mother's voice was suddenly much sharper. Alison's eyes must have looked glazed.

She was listening all right. But inside her head the gears were turning. She had never seen her mother so vulnerable. The translucent skin under her eyes was puffy. Alison wondered if she cried at night. If the other prisoners were nice to her. If they were afraid of her or if she was afraid of them.

"The tables have turned. This is war. I need to know you are on my side." Helen's image in the glass blended with Alison's own reflection. Neither of them showed any emotion. "Tamara is playing with fire, and this time she is the one who is going to get burned." Helen sounded certain. Alison was not so sure.

She stuck her free hand in the pocket of her jacket and felt the tiny glass figurine she had taken the other day at Zoey's. She wasn't sure why she had taken it. She hadn't stolen anything in a long time. She used to do it a lot, especially when her mom was on her case. It was comforting – some small thing that she alone could control. Maybe that was why she had done it the other day, when everything was spinning wildly away from her. Seeing her mom's arraignment on TV in front of Tom and Zoey had pushed her over some new edge. Ever since her mom's arrest, she'd felt like she was falling, and each time she thought she was about to hit the bottom it would move to some deeper, darker place and the fall would go on. Inside her pocket, Alison snapped the delicate figure in two.

"Why, Mom?" Alison asked. "Why would Grandmother do that?" She was not sure what to believe. There were so many lies going back so far she was not sure she could sort them out, or if she even needed to. She had been so dumb. Kelly's ruthlessness should not have come as such a shock. It was what she was born to do. Alison had been crazy to think her cousin would stand by her.

Now it was all becoming clear. The Diamonds stood by no one, especially not one another. Until now, Alison had managed to stay just outside the cruel games and conniving ways. Well, maybe not always, but she had managed to stay upright while her mother and grandmother slid her back and forth across the game board like a pawn. Now, suddenly, the stakes were higher.

"It's complicated, Alison. All you need to know is that I'm counting on you to help. You're my daughter," Helen went on stating facts. It was what she did when she was afraid. You couldn't argue with facts. Alison simply stared, rubbing her thumb along the jagged edge of the elephant trunk in her pocket. As she gazed upon the image of her face reflected in the glass, with her mother's face ghostlike behind it, she felt something shift. For the first time Alison was more than a pawn. She was a player. Whether she was right about Grandmother Diamond or not, her mother needed her. And the next move was Alison's.

Chapter 18

Slumping at the smallest table in Hardwired, Zoey scowled out at the world. Her nasty look was wasted on the coffee crowd. They were too wrapped up in their lattes and newspapers to notice, but she wanted to hone her evil stare before turning it on her dad's tutor. As far as she was concerned, this guy was not her tutor. He belonged exclusively to her father, who hired him.

Studying with a tutor was the last thing Zoey wanted to do on a Thursday night. First of all, it wasn't like the classes at Stafford were hard for her. The course load was a joke compared to the work she'd had to do at boarding school. And second, meeting a tutor was a waste of time. Time that could be spent on more important things – like taking down Alison Rose.

Checking the door again for any sign of a professional nerd, Zoey flipped open her laptop and reread the latest email from Alison.

Zo –

Greetings from study hall. It's so boring here I can feel myself slipping into a coma. People are looking at me like I'm last week's lunch special. Thank GOD you came home from boarding school when you did. I needed a friend. Don't know what I'd do without you.

    Love,

    A

    PS Why did you come back, anyway?

"To repay a little debt," Zoey muttered. Thanks to Kelly and Chad, and her mom's arrest, Alison was in full free fall, and Zoey was the only person in the world she trusted. Ripping away her safety net was going to be easy. And fun. Finally she would know what it was like to be abandoned at the moment you needed someone the most. Zoey's chest tightened and she took a gulp of her latte, forcing down the scalding-hot liquid along with the painful memory of the loneliest night of her life. The night she had lost so much more than her best friend. She took another, slower sip, letting the hot liquid cool on her tongue. *Focus on the payback,* she reminded herself.

    Her old friend was going to go up in flames . . . like so many other things in Zoey's life. Zoey forced a laugh as images of her last school flickered in her mind. That disaster had been an accident. This one would not be.

    "What's so funny?"

    Zoey slapped her laptop shut and looked up, prepared to tell the person standing over her to bug off. Then she saw him. He was in college, for sure. Longish hair, vintage jeans, V-neck, easy smile. Totally hot.

"Are you Zoey?" he asked without waiting for an answer to his first question. Zoey nodded dumbly and the guy sat down. "Jeremy." He held out his hand, and Zoey shook it. Usually she felt dumb shaking hands. But with Jeremy it was OK. His hand was big and warm – not sweaty or anything, just warm. She felt a tingle make its way up her arm.

"Are you the tutor?" Zoey asked. She was planning to say "my dad's" tutor but didn't. It wasn't this guy's fault her dad was so lame, right? Besides, his Abercrombie good looks were putting her in a forgiving mood.

Jeremy smiled, revealing perfect teeth and dimples. "You got it," he said. "So what do we need to work on?"

How are you at revenge? Zoey thought. Aloud she said, "Nothing really. It's not like I'm failing. My dad's just afraid I'm going to get kicked out again." She hoped that sounded kind of cool.

"Again?" Jeremy didn't miss a trick.

"Fifth time," Zoey confessed. She wasn't sure why. Maybe it was the dimples.

"Huh," Jeremy said, giving Zoey a once-over, then leaning in to study her face. "Cutting class?"

It was a good guess. She had been cutting, kind of. But that wasn't the reason she'd been expelled . . . this time. For a split second she considered telling him the whole story. Then her sense returned. "Let's just say I was the one who got burned and leave it at that." Zoey hoped that would be the end of it. Luckily Jeremy was too smart to press further. Instead he offered to get her something to go with her coffee.

"So how is it being home?" Jeremy asked when he returned with a macchiato and a brownie to share. "How are you doing?"

Zoey swallowed hard and shrugged. Jeremy was the first person who had asked her that since she'd arrived home. "Not great," Zoey confessed, surprising herself. What was it about this guy that made her jaw flap? "I mean, my brother is acting weird. We used to be close but now we barely speak. My dad is running for Congress, so he's even more uptight than usual. And the only person I hang out with is this girl, Alison Rose, who's—"

"Wait. You mean Helen Rose's daughter?" Jeremy's already big eyes grew bigger. "Wow." He pushed his thick, dark hair off his forehead and held a handful of it for a minute like she had just told him something amazing.

"Yeah, that Alison Rose." Zoey sat back and looked at Jeremy in silence. He didn't seem like the stupid starstruck type. What was his deal?

"I, uh, my mom loves Helen Rose stuff," Jeremy said quickly, dropping his hand. "You should see my dorm room – everything Helen. But you were saying. . ."

"Well, Alison and I were supertight in fifth grade—"

"So, what's she like?" Jeremy interrupted. He took a sip of his drink and wiped the steamed milk foam off his lip before leaning even closer.

Zoey was not sure how much she wanted to reveal about Alison or why Jeremy wanted to know. Was he out for the Rose gossip? She had to reel it in a bit. "You know, she's like, a . . . girl," she said. She was about to say Alison was "normal", but that was far from the truth. No one in Alison's family was "normal". Nor was Jeremy's interest in Alison. "So how do *you* like Silver Spring? You just here for school?" Zoey changed the subject.

Jeremy seemed to understand immediately. "Yeah. School." He nodded. "And as for Silver Spring . . . it's got potential." Jeremy smiled again and all was forgiven. There was something really familiar about his eyes. "So, do you have any homework?" he asked. "Maybe that's a good place to start."

Chapter 19

Kelly switched her mobile to "silent" before entering Grandma D's house. Her Highness hated interruptions, especially mobiles. She operated strictly on dinosaur time – no computers, no mobiles, no microwave – nothing that beeped. She could have a smart house if she wanted to, with walls that moved and music that followed you and security up the wazoo. But she preferred hoarding to spending.

"Kelly. You're late." Grandmother Diamond was sitting in her parlour holding court when Kelly walked in. She looked every bit the queen, swirling a crystal glass of tinkling ice instead of a sceptre. Her loyal subjects were there, too. Well, most of them.

Phoebe and Bill, Kelly's mom and dad, sat at the inlaid gaming table looking like something out of a Brooks Brothers catalogue. They held hands and smiled politely, standing to greet their daughter. Kelly knew her mom was hoping she would come kiss her on the cheek to make her look good in front of Her Highness. She also knew if she didn't, her dad would lay into her about it when she got home. But she didn't feel like it, so she waved casually. "Mumsy. Pops." She smiled as her mother's face fell.

In front of Kelly, Aunt Christine was standing behind the settee checking her reflection in the huge framed mirror. Probably checking for new lines to shoot with Botox. If she wasn't careful she might reveal an emotion. Pausing in her inspection, Christine turned around. "Nice of you to join us," she said snidely. Then she leaned in so Kelly could kiss the air near her cheek.

Nice of you to point out I'm late, Kelly thought. It was already obvious she was the last one to arrive.

Alison had even managed to make it without a driver. She was seated right next to Her Highness, huddling under her wing. A few weeks ago Kelly and Alison would have been speaking in eyebrows and furtive text messages, planning their getaway to the pool house. Tonight, however, her cousin was carefully avoiding her gaze.

"Now that you're finally here, we can go in to dinner . . . assuming it's not cold." Grandmother Diamond stood stiffly and led the way to the dining room with the help of a carved gold cane Kelly had never seen before. As far as she knew, her grandmother did not have a problem walking. Probably just for show.

The table was laid with creamy china ringed in gold and set with the full complement of silver. The old stuff, Kelly noticed. Taking her usual seat on her grandmother's left,

Kelly arranged her napkin on her lap and her smile on her face. It was time to remind Alison of all she had recently lost. "Aunt Christine, I love those earrings. Are they Harry Winston?" she asked sweetly.

Christine reached up and touched the huge diamonds dangling from her ears as if she had forgotten she was wearing them. "Oh, these. Aren't they divine? They're worth a fortune, of course."

Kelly glanced at Alison. She was keeping up the stoic thing pretty well. Impressive – and irritating. Her facade needed cracking.

"Those would be perfect with the dress I bought for the autumn formal tomorrow," Kelly went on. "Don't you think dangly and slinky are perfect together?"

Alison ignored the comment and delicately spooned up a bite of lobster bisque. Her table manners were infuriatingly perfect – far better than Kelly's, as Her Highness liked to remind her.

"I'm sure you'll find something," Aunt Christine said dismissively.

Kelly scowled. That wasn't the answer she was looking for. "Chad is going to flip when he sees me in that dress," she said. "You know, it's funny, he's even more excited about this dance than I am." Before Kelly could survey the damage, her mom piped in and added to it.

"You're going to the dance, too, aren't you, dear?" Phoebe looked at Alison expectantly. Kelly tried not to choke on her soup – this was richer than the bisque. Alison merely shook her head.

"Kelly, do stop slouching." Her Highness spoiled the mood with the usual tongue-lashing. "It's so unbecoming."

Kelly straightened but her scowl returned. Couldn't her grandmother leave her alone for one second? And what was it with her and Alison, anyway? They were acting tighter than ever. Did Alison forget it was Her Highness who framed her mom? Didn't she care? Kelly stopped eating. They were hypocrites, both of them. As far as she was concerned, they deserved each other.

Just then one of Tamara's servants came into the dining room and whispered something in her ear. "You'll have to excuse me for a few moments," Tamara said as she got to her feet and walked out of the room. Kelly was extremely curious – it was rare for her grandmother to allow an interruption at meal time – but her grandmother's face was a mask.

As soon as the old woman was out of the room, Aunt Christine changed the subject again. "I heard you went to see your mother, Alison. How is she?" she said. "Prison must be ghastly."

Alison paled and stuck a big bite of food in her mouth. Kelly recognized the strategy. She was buying time to think. Can't talk with your mouth full.

Alison chewed slowly and thoroughly. "She's doing great," she finally said. "It's pretty posh there, really, one of those white-collar prisons, you know? Practically a country club. She gets to read a lot and exercise. I think she's even lost a little weight."

Phoebe clutched her napkin. "Oh, I am so glad to hear that," she gushed.

Kelly stared at her mom. She was so gullible. Couldn't she see that Alison was lying? The poor girl wasn't even very good at it.

"I have not been sleeping nights worrying about her . . . and you, Alison," Kelly's mom went on. She loved to play the good mommy. "I just hope this whole thing will blow over and maybe even bring the family back together. Perhaps Mother will even put Helen back on the list."

Kelly's father coughed. "I wouldn't go that far," he said. Then he glanced at Alison. "Though we're all concerned about Helen." Across the table, Alison was studying her soup again.

Aunt Christine smiled into her napkin. "Yes, very concerned. But I doubt Mother will keep a criminal in her will."

Kelly bit her tongue to keep from laughing.

"Is that all you can think about?" Grandmother Diamond strode back into the room, her cane never touching the floor. Sitting down, she glared at the people seated at her polished mahogany table – her family. "What I do with my money is my business. If that is all you are here for, you can see yourselves to the door." She gestured to the foyer on the other side of the archway. When nobody moved, she nodded and took a long drink of wine.

"You are all nothing but a pack of ungrateful, money-grubbing leeches," she hissed, setting the wine glass down.

"Tamara, we haven't borrowed a cent from you in years," Kelly's dad tried to defend himself. If she could have reached his knee from where she was sitting, Kelly would have kicked it. It may have been a long time, but Kelly knew her dad had borrowed money in the past, and anyone who had ever borrowed money from Tamara never escaped Her Highness's debt. Grandmother Diamond kept track of what was owed her more meticulously than the IRS – and that included more than just money.

"No you haven't, have you, Bill?" Grandmother Diamond spoke softly, then went for the kill. "Instead of borrowing what you didn't have, you've charged it and racked up incredible debt that Christine had to bail you out of. You think I don't know? And who do you think will pay it off next time? I hope you aren't planning to saddle my daughter – or my granddaughter – with that when you die. I certainly never would."

Kelly's dad turned red and went silent.

"And it's your fault for marrying him." Grandmother Diamond glared at Kelly's mom, who recoiled like a kicked puppy.

"Well, you don't have to worry about *me*. I'm holding my own, Mother." Aunt Christine used her best "offended" voice and jabbed at her salad with a perfectly polished sterling silver fork. "We're all doing OK, except Little Miss Rose over there. She's the family charity case." Aunt Christine laughed as if she meant it as a joke. But Kelly could see from Alison's face that the zinger had hit its mark.

"Alison is not a charity case," Grandmother Diamond chastised her daughter. "Her family has simply fallen on hard times."

Hard times. "Thanks to you," Kelly mumbled just loud enough for Alison to hear. She was furious. She could not believe Grandmother Diamond was taking Alison's side on this. It just didn't make sense to her that Tamara could be mad enough at her own daughter to send her to jail and yet remain so attached to Alison.

"So how *are* you handling these hard times, Alison? Do you miss your mother very much?" Kelly sat up straight and proper in a perfect imitation of Her Highness. "Of course, you must be furious at whoever turned her in, or framed her. I mean, your mother *is* innocent, right?"

Alison looked straight at Kelly, as expressionless as a professional poker player. "Of course she is. Helen Rose doesn't make mistakes." The mention of Helen's name in front of Tamara made everyone suck in a little breath. It had been unuttered before Her Highness for so long. And claiming that she didn't make mistakes? What was that? Alison was asking for it.

Kelly seethed silently at Alison's lack of anger. Why wasn't she furious? How could she forgive her grandmother for doing such a horrible thing to her mother? And Grandma D would be all over her if Kelly made remarks like that. . .

Slowly it began to dawn on Kelly. Alison was not just seeking out Her Highness's protection, she had the old lady in her pocket. More important, Alison was *not* missing her mother. Nobody knew better than Kelly how much those two fought. Alison had Grandmother Diamond on her side, and whether it was intentional or not, the old bat had done Alison a favour. She'd eliminated Alison's enemy number one. She had got rid of monster mom Helen Rose.

Chapter 20

Alison kicked her overflowing laundry basket and fell to the floor with a yelp to nurse her stubbed toe. She made a mental note never to kick anything in flip-flops again. Elise had stopped showing up since they couldn't pay her, and the house was a wreck. Everywhere there were signs that things were not normal. Newspapers sat on the driveway. Dead flowers rotted in the vases. Flat couch pillows went unfluffed. And there were enough dust bunnies skittering about that if they banded together they could probably take over. Alison's dad certainly wouldn't put up much of a fight – he had only been getting dressed to go to the country club, and Alison had noticed that he usually just wore the same shirt. By five thirty he was home, usually tipsy, and flopped in front of the TV. He'd worn a groove in the leather sofa and eaten every bit of prepackaged food from the freezer. He might as well be waving a white flag of surrender. He and Alison hadn't had a conversation since she didn't know when.

If Helen got out of prison unexpectedly, the shock of seeing her husband and perfect home in such a state would probably kill her. Alison smiled at the thought before grabbing an armful of dirty jeans and staggering down the hall to the laundry room. She did not want to do laundry – in fact, she wasn't even sure she could figure out how – but her dad wasn't going to and she needed something to wear.

She shoved the load into the machine, dumped in some soap, pushed "normal", and hoped everything would work out. Water poured into the machine, and Alison turned to leave, satisfied. Then she noticed what was hanging on the back of the laundry room door. It was the BCBG halter dress she had got about a month ago to wear to the autumn formal tonight. It hung forlornly, waiting for an iron that would never come.

The dress was perfect. Even her mother had agreed. And the dance plans had all been set. She, Chad, Kelly and Tom were going to share a limo. They were going to have sushi. They were going to stand up through the sunroof in the back of the long black car and drive through town screaming at the top of their lungs. They were going to eat and dance and laugh. Only instead she was here, alone, at her falling-apart home, washing dirty denim.

Alison reached out and felt the silky hem of the dress. Kelly and Chad were still going to the formal. Together, she knew, since Kelly had been kind enough to mention it several times the night before. Tom probably had a date, too. They were probably all getting ready right now. . .

Suddenly the dress hanging on the door looked a little blurry, and Alison found herself slumping. Right in the middle of the laundry room floor, she suddenly fell apart. It was all too much. Too, too much.

She knew it was stupid to miss people who had been so mean to her. But Alison felt more alone than she had in her whole life. She ached with it. And the person she was loneliest for was the person who had caused this nightmare: Kelly.

Pulling herself together, Alison grabbed her mobile. She scrolled through the long list of numbers – none of which she called any more. Zoey Ramirez was at the bottom. She hit "send" and then hung up almost immediately. Zoey had a tutoring appointment. Or at least that's what she'd said. She was probably going to the dance, too, and didn't want Alison to feel bad.

"Ugh." Alison shoved her phone in her pocket and stumbled down the hall to the kitchen. The moment she stepped on the marble floor she knew it was a mistake.

"Hi, Dad," she mumbled. Her father was slumped at the counter looking blearily at a stack of mail and drinking something that looked like iced tea and smelled like rubbing alcohol.

"Hmph," her father greeted her without looking up.

"Everything OK?" Alison ventured, not really wanting to hear the answer.

"Our accountant quit. I can't deal with this garbage." Her father threw up his hands, almost knocking his drink and the bills off the counter. "Everyone wants money. Do you have any idea what we pay for your school?" he asked accusingly.

Alison did not have a clue and didn't really want to. She'd never had to think about anything like that . . . until now. Her father shuffled through the stack of bills until he located one on Stafford letterhead. It was too late to back out of the room. Alison took it from him and looked at the number in red and then the due date. Her tuition was due a week ago – and the figure was huge.

"They called yesterday. I asked for a little more time but. . ." Jack Rose let the words die in his mouth. Alison could guess the rest. The daughter of a criminal was one thing. The freeloading daughter of a criminal was another. She was about to be kicked out of school.

"All we ever wanted was the best for you." Her dad was slurring and his voice sounded wet. He was drunk and skipping right over the angry part to the weepy part. Alison knew she had to get out of there. Now.

"Don't worry about it, Dad," she said lightly. "I'm going to Kelly's tonight, but we can talk about it in the morning." Alison ducked quickly out of the kitchen before her dad could say another word. He had no clue about what was going on with her and Kelly, but why she had said she was going to her cousin's house was beyond her. It almost sounded fun . . . until she recalled everything that had happened and what Kelly was really doing tonight, with *her* boyfriend.

Throwing the few clean things she had left in her drawers into a LeSportsac duffel along with the school bill she still had in her hand, Alison tiptoed back downstairs. Her dad's suit jacket hung over the banister. She silently felt the pockets until she found his wallet. Slipping out all of the bills, she pushed them into the pocket of her hoodie. Then she yelled, "Goodbye," and sprinted out the door. She had no idea where she was going; she just knew she could not stay in that house one minute longer.

Chapter 21

WUNDERTWIN1. Tom typed in his password and waited for his dad's computer to retrieve his email. The connection seemed slow, so while the cursor spun he clicked on his father's desktop files. There was a document about a case he was working on, a partially written campaign speech (drafted by some lackey, no doubt), and another document marked CONFIDENTIAL. That looked interesting. . .

Tom leaned closer to the screen, reading carefully. The letter had to do with his bid for Congress and included a list of potential campaign donors. Tom recognized most of the names, but one in particular caught his eye – Tamara Diamond. She had the cash, all right.

The computer chimed, letting him know his mail was in, but he ignored it as he eyed the list. Then the doorbell rang. Chad was early.

Bummer, Tom thought. He would have to finish the report another time. Right now he had a hot date as a third wheel – he was off to the dance with Chad and Kelly.

Normally Tom was not the third-wheel type. There were plenty of girls who would have loved to be his date to the formal. But since the only date he wanted was Kelly, and since Kelly was his best friend's girl, well, he had no choice but to tag along. For now.

"Calm down," Tom called as the doorball rang a second time. He straightened his jacket and yanked open the door.

The girl on the doorstep smiled sheepishly. "Hey."

Tom smiled back, confused. "Alison. What are you doing here?" he asked. Then, because that sounded kind of rude, he tried again. "I mean, I was expect – I wasn't expecting you. Zoey's not here."

"Right. I knew that." Alison hit her forehead with her palm. "And you –" Alison looked Tom up and down, admiring his Hugo Boss suit – "are clearly off to the dance."

Tom wished it weren't so obvious. Way back when, before Alison's mom was arrested and Kelly stole Chad, and Alison fell way, way off the A-list, Alison was supposed to be going with them to the dance. Tom wished he could turn back time . . . for a couple of reasons. The first was blonde and beautiful – and would have been his date for the dance by default. He'd had a better chance at snagging Kelly when she wasn't on Chad's arm. The second was the brunette standing on his front porch.

He would never say it to Kelly or Chad, but Tom felt bad for Alison, especially after seeing her face when the news came on the other day. He couldn't believe Zoey had made her watch that. It was so rude and embarrassing. For most of the people in Silver Spring it was a delicious scandal, but for Helen Rose and her daughter it was a long, hard fall from grace. And Zoey seemed to think that Alison deserved it.

Tom could not figure out his sister. First she acted like Alison never stopped being her best friend when they both knew the girl had turned on her in the worst possible way on the worse possible night . . . the night their mom had died in a car crash. Now Alison seemed to be the only friend Zoey had, but then Zoey pulled a stunt like that. Did she like Alison or hate her?

"So, is Zoey going, too?" Alison asked. "After her tutoring session?" She was still standing on the porch looking a little embarrassed. Like some school kid selling magazine subscriptions.

"Uh, no. Um. Do you want to come in?" Tom looked over Alison's shoulder, hoping she would say no, hoping Chad and the limo would be late. This could get really awkward. As if it weren't already. "The dance isn't really Zoey's scene. I don't know when she's coming back, but you can wait for her if you want."

"That would be great." Alison looked relieved, and beat. She followed Tom into the living room and slumped down on the couch beside her bag. It looked like she had brought enough stuff to stay for a week.

"Where are you going?" Tom asked, pointing at the duffel. *And how did you get here?* he wondered. There was no car in the drive when she rang the bell.

"I, uh. . ." Alison looked at her bag like she had never seen it before. "I guess I don't know," she said quietly.

In her capris and Pumas, she was not dressed to go out, but Tom suddenly wished he could invite her along to the formal as his date. Then he stepped back into reality. If the scene in the living room right now was awkward, the scene in the limo with Chad and Kelly would be torturous. Not to mention the fact that being nice to Alison in public . . . well, it wasn't going to happen. Tom was not ready to jump off that bridge.

"Uh, Zoey should be here soon. I think." Tom tossed the TV remote on to the couch near Alison's hand. "Debbie . . . I mean, Deirdre is upstairs if you need anything." Alison just kept looking at him. Blinking.

"I think I'm just going to wait outside," Tom said. Backing slowly out of the room, he felt like he was making a desperate escape – like Alison was a wounded animal that might attack. He went out the front door and sat on the step. When the limo pulled into the circular drive he breathed a sigh of relief and hurried for the door before anyone could get out. Time to turn his attention to the night at hand – and his best friend's girlfriend.

Chapter 22

Lightning flashed in Alison's dream. One moment she was in the lunchroom at Stafford, eating alone on a platform high above the other students. The next she was caught in a storm inside the school. Still at her high table, she felt the rain begin and heard the laughter of the other students. She was on display and would not be allowed down until she ate all of the food on her tray. But the food was writhing. She could barely pick it up, let alone choke it down. Lightning flashed again and Alison opened her eyes and sat up.

"Look who's up." Kelly stood in the doorway of Grandma D's pool house with her mobile in her hand. "Hello, Sleeping Beauty," she sneered.

Remembering where she was, Alison felt her blood go cold. She had arrived after midnight – it was a long walk from Zoey's – punched in the alarm code on the back gate, and let herself into the pool house. She could not think of anywhere else to go and had hoped no one would find her – at least not until morning.

Alison stared at Kelly. She was still wearing her sequined

dress and Prada heels. She looked great. And Alison looked. . . Oh. It was bad.

Alison was dressed in sweats. She was wrapped in her old pink unicorns-and-rainbows sleeping bag, and there were probably streaks of black mascara on her cheeks. Rubbing her finger under her eyes, she looked down and shoved her old stuffed dog deeper into the bag. He was still a little wet from her tears. It was the only way Alison could get to sleep these days.

"What are you doing here?" Alison gulped. She was trying to sound fierce or accusing. Instead she sounded like a surprised kid in a sleeping bag.

"We just stopped by for a little private after-party," Kelly said casually.

Oh, no. Kelly said "we". As that idea sank in, Chad's face appeared at Kelly's side. Then Tom's. They looked surprised to see her, and worse, they looked like they felt sorry for her.

Alison struggled to stand up but was too wrapped in her bag. She fell over, caught herself, and ended up crawling across the floor to kick free.

"Smooth." Kelly's giggles echoed in Alison's ears.

Taking a deep breath, Alison stood up. She wasn't going down without a fight. "Hi, guys," she said casually. "I didn't realize this was a sleepover."

"It's not," Kelly said snidely.

"Pool party, then?" Alison kept smiling. She reached into

her bag and pulled out her swimsuit. Her cousin looked a little stunned – like she'd been expecting Alison to just lie there and be humiliated.

As she slipped into the bathroom and closed the door, Alison's heart was pounding. Kelly had the upper hand when they were at school, but this was family turf and Alison was determined to hold her own.

She pulled her dark hair into a short ponytail and adjusted her tankini, grateful she had shoved it into her duffel. It had broad brown and green stripes. It looked great on her and she knew it. She emerged from the bathroom ready to make a splash. Kelly, Chad, and Tom were still fully dressed and standing by the door.

"So, Chip, how about a dip?" Alison punched Tom lightly on the shoulder as she squeezed past him into the warm, dark night air. It was an old joke between her and Kelly. Without pausing to see if anyone was going to join her, Alison walked to the diving board and climbed the short ladder. She stood for a moment near the steps, then took three long strides, jumped once, arced out over the water, and sliced into it easily with barely a splash. She knew it was a good dive as soon as she left the board and was grateful for all the swimming lessons her mother had insisted upon. When she pulled herself up at the side of the pool, Tom was clapping. Kelly shushed him, but Alison bowed her head and held up a hand, soaking in the applause. "You should see my cannonball." She laughed.

"That sounds like a challenge." Tom looked at Alison slyly and started loosening his tie.

Kelly gave Tom a withering look. "You're not going in."

If he heard her, Tom did not let on. He marched to the diving board in his boxer shorts, jumped once on the end, tucked his knees, and smacked down into the water, sending up a mini tidal wave. Kelly stepped out of the way of the splash, but Chad got soaked.

"Dude, you did not just do that." Chad was smiling as he looked at his dripping trousers. "Might as well go in now." He shrugged apologetically at Kelly and pulled off his jacket and shirt.

Alison hid her smile. Two down. "Come on in, Kel, water's fine," Alison coaxed. Kicking off from the side of the pool, she did a perfect backstroke towards the hot tub.

"Fine." Kelly turned in a huff. Alison knew this was not going as Kelly had planned. She also knew there was no way Kelly would get in the pool in her underwear. She kept a suit in the pool house. "But I'm only getting in the hot tub."

"There's a hot tub?" Tom asked.

"Yup," Alison called from across the pool. She slid into the water and fired the jets. It was so hot she had to catch her breath. But it felt great – almost as good as making Kelly do something she didn't want to.

"Ow. Ow. Ow. How can you stand this heat?" Tom flinched, making faces as he stepped into the whirlpool.

"Oh, you get used to it." Alison laughed easily and Tom joined her. She wasn't sure if he knew she was talking about the burns she had got from Kelly, but it felt great to laugh about it.

"Got room for me?" Chad stood on the edge of the hot tub between Tom and Alison and waited for Tom to move over so he could sit between them. Was he getting jealous?

"So how was the dance?" Alison asked. She wanted to make sure the three of them looked like they were having a good time when Kelly came back out of the pool house.

Chad shrugged. "OK, I guess. You didn't miss much."

But she had, really. She had missed him and being a part of the crowd.

"You should have seen Nelson and Kaminski on the dance floor, though." Tom stood up and did an imitation of their PE teacher slow dancing with their geometry teacher, his arms wrapped all the way around himself so he was playing with his own hair.

Chad cracked up, putting his head really, really close to Alison's shoulder. "I wish you could have seen it." He laughed.

"I just wanted to relax tonight." Alison shrugged, still grinning. "It's been a rough week."

"You can say that again." Chad's smile faded. He was looking right into Alison's blue eyes and she could tell what he was thinking – that he was sorry for whatever part he'd played in making her life difficult. Alison waited, hoping he would say it, but what happened next was even better. Kelly emerged just in time to catch them gazing at each other. Tom waved her over, but Chad didn't look away.

"Al, I'm really. . ." Chad stumbled on his own tongue.

Out of the corner of her eye, Alison watched Kelly approach. She stepped into the tub, squealing at the heat, and settled between Alison and Chad. The tub went silent.

"Don't let me break up the party," Kelly sniped. She put Chad's arm around her shoulders. "Miss me?"

"Not much," Alison said brightly. Her work here was done. Now it was playtime. "Double cannonball?" she asked Tom, checking to see if Chad was paying attention. He was.

"Oh, yeah!" Another great thing about Tom – he was up for anything. They were on the board about to jump when Alison's heart stopped for the second time that night.

Grandmother Diamond was standing on the deck with her arms crossed. Alison could tell by her posture that she was glaring at them.

"Cannonball!" Tom yelled. His splash was enormous, but not loud enough to cover Grandmother Diamond's booming voice.

"Get out of my pool this instant! Kelly! Alison! You should be ashamed of yourselves. I was about to call the police. You're lucky I didn't have you arrested!"

"Like the rest of the family?" Alison said before she could stop herself. Her grandmother looked at her sharply, then looked away as if she hadn't heard anything.

"I thought you were intruders," Grandmother Diamond went on, glaring at Kelly. Chad cowered behind her, and Tom was now out of the pool, shivering in the night air. "You *are* intruders. And I want you all dressed and out of here immediately."

Alison hesitated. She glanced at Kelly, then looked at her bare feet. "I'm so sorry, Grandmother. I should have called to tell you I was coming. I was just sleeping in the pool house. Our place is so empty . . . and then when Kelly showed up with the guys, well . . . we didn't mean to disturb you. It was inconsiderate of us, I know. I guess I'm under a lot of stress." She raised her eyes to meet her grandmother's. "Can I stay? Your house is the only place that feels like home."

Tamara Diamond's expression relaxed. Alison could feel her anger softening, like melting ice cream. She had laid it on extra thick for Kelly's benefit.

"Of course you may stay." Grandmother Diamond smiled at her granddaughter affectionately. "But the rest of you have to go. Kelly, I am calling your parents as soon as I get back into the house." Alison smiled. That phone call was icing on the cake. Aunt Phoebe would be mortified by her mother's anger, and Kelly would get a lengthy lecture. She would pretend to ignore it but. . .

Alison didn't even have to look up to know Kelly was already fuming. The heat coming off that girl was intense. She was a volcano about to blow.

Alison scampered up to the boys and gave each of them a peck on the cheek. "Thanks for coming, guys!" she bubbled. Then she waved at her cousin's retreating back. "Love you, Kel. See you Monday!"

Chapter 23

Kelly slammed the door to her bedroom, half wishing it would crack the plaster. The ride back to her house in the limo was awkward, and Chad had seemed . . . irritated. Kelly had insisted on being dropped off first, just to get it over with.

Once she got inside, things got even worse. Her mother was sitting like a statue on the sofa while her father paced back and forth in his Ralph Lauren sheepskin slippers.

"This is the last straw," her father said, his voice kind of shaky. He never was good at discipline.

"Your grandmother was very upset," her mother added. "She thought she was being robbed!"

"She thought we were robbing the hot tub? I wasn't the first one there," Kelly said. "And the midnight swim was Alison's idea!"

"Really," Phoebe said, raising an eyebrow. "And did Alison bring boys to the pool?" she asked pointedly. "I understand she's staying the weekend at Mother's, so of course she was the first one there. Honestly, Kelly. The way you insist on blaming everything on Alison when you know she is having a tough time. . ."

Kelly had stood there saying nothing while her mother waited for an apology that would never come. Finally she'd been dismissed.

Face up and arms crossed, Kelly flopped on to her down duvet. The last straw was Alison waving goodbye like a cheerleader. Not to mention the simpering look on her face when she was weaselling up to Her Highness. It was disgusting. It was shameless. And Kelly knew the show was all for her. Alison loved to rub her nose in the fact that she was their grandmother's favourite – Tamara's little lap dog. It made Kelly sick.

Ugh! Kelly rolled over. She hated pouting. It was useless. She much preferred to turn her hurt into anger. Being mad helped her focus.

Only in this case Kelly wasn't sure she had the power to change anything. No matter how far under Kelly pulled her, Alison bobbed right back to the surface like Ivory soap. It really burned Kelly up. Apparently she and her aunt Christine were the only people in the world who could see past Alison's goody-goody charms.

Even Chad was still susceptible. Kelly could have sworn she saw the word "sorry" starting to form on her boy's lips in the hot tub. He had nothing to be sorry for! Was he sorry he was with her, the most popular girl in school? Was he sorry Alison was so pathetic? Chad was weak. She was going to have to watch him – to make sure he didn't go astray.

Kelly stood up and grabbed her purse off the floor. "If you wanted to make me mad, Al, you did," she said under her breath. "And if you're wondering how much it's going to cost you. . ." Kelly grimaced as she flipped open her phone and looked at the hideous picture she had taken of poor little Alison curled up in her unicorn-covered sleeping bag, hugging her stuffed puppy. Kelly scrolled down and selected "send". If a picture spoke a thousand words, how many words did hundreds of pictures speak? Alison would know soon enough. The photo would spread like wildfire.

Feeling a little bit satisfied, Kelly moved on to the other person who was getting on her nerves. She turned her computer on and quickly searched for a phone number online. A few seconds later she was dialling the number. "Oh, hello?" she said sweetly, watching her face in the mirror and sharing the joke with her reflection. "Sorry to call so late. I'm trying to reach Zoey. Yeah. Zoey Ramirez." The voice on the other end of the line was groggy. "She's not in your dorm any more? Is she still at the school? She's not? What happened?" Groggy voice was all too willing to fill her in. "She was kicked out for *what*? Oh my gosh."

Kelly had to hold back a laugh as Grog spilled all the details. This was going to be way better than she'd ever thought possible.

Chapter 24

Reaching for another photo album from the stack on the coffee table, Alison stifled a yawn. It was almost two in the morning, but she couldn't sleep. She flipped the album open. She and Kelly were on almost every page, as babies, girls on horseback, at birthdays. . . Pressing on her stomach to stop the dull ache that had been growing there, she turned the page. More little Kellys and Alisons with their hair in braids smiled up at her.

She smiled back at the pictures. She missed that Kelly – the one she'd grown up with. They were like sisters. They had shared everything. Until they shared Chad.

Alison wondered if things would ever be like they were before. If she would ever get *her* Kelly back. The dull ache tightened into a sharper pain. Probably not. Not after everything that had happened. Alison certainly was not ready to forgive her. She shoved aside that album and picked up an older one. She didn't need those memories right now. Flipping open the album, Alison stopped abruptly and stared.

The photo that had caught her eye showed three young women posing by the side of the pool. They were squinting into the sun, but it was easy for Alison to recognize her mother. She wondered why she had never seen the photo before. Grandma D had removed all the pictures of her mother from the Diamond family archives long ago. But there was her mom, hugely pregnant, standing with her sisters. And Helen was not the only pregnant sister, either. Beside her, Aunt Christine looked like she was smuggling a watermelon under her dress.

Alison did a double take. She could feel her blood rushing faster in her veins. It did not make any sense. Aunt Christine did not have any children. Or did she?

Chapter 25

The next morning at breakfast, Alison poked the yolk of her egg and watched it bleed on to the white china plate. Next to her, tucked under her butter knife, lay the tuition letter from Stafford. She had tested her acting skills last night by the pool – but that was just the rehearsal for this morning's performance.

"Seeing her at the jail. . ." Alison waited until her grandmother's mouth was full before she spoke. She wanted to make sure she was not interrupted too quickly. "It was just awful. I hope I never have to see her like that again – in that place. I mean. . ." Twisting her napkin into a pretzel for effect, Alison counted to five before she continued. She wanted to make sure her grandmother was listening. "She used to be so strong. Like you. She built herself up from nothing."

Taking a bite of dry toast, Alison chewed delicately and washed it down with a sip of juice. She'd been rehearsing this little speech since she'd woken up and was pleased to finally be able to recite it. Normally Alison did not dare bring up her mother at her grandmother's house. But things had not been normal for a long time. And she was quite certain that there was a bit of pride attached to all of Tamara's anger.

"First of all," Grandmother Diamond began, "Honey did not build herself up from nothing. She began as a Diamond. Your mother had a fine upbringing and could have had anything she wanted if she had not been too proud to ask." Tamara picked up her coffee cup and set it down without taking a drink. Her spoon clattered off the saucer on to the polished table. Alison held her breath waiting for her grandmother to say more. She had to say more.

"Secondly. . ." Grandmother Diamond leaned closer. Alison could have counted the gems in her encrusted earrings if she wanted to. "I want you to tell me what good her money is doing her now. Hmmm? What good is it doing any of you?"

"No good at all." Alison shook her head.

"Not like my money," Tamara said, straightening. "And I would rather be buried with it than see it in ungrateful hands." Grandmother Diamond narrowed her eyes. "Your mother took a gamble, Alison. A foolish gamble. She bet that she didn't need her family, didn't need her mother's support. She thought she could build her own fortune, her own fortress, her own reputation. She was wrong. Your family is your foundation, Alison – without it . . . you will crumble."

"Yes, Grandmother," Alison said. "You know how grateful I am for all you have done for me."

Grandmother Diamond patted Alison's hand. "Don't you worry. The Diamonds have always been well respected. With your mother out of the picture we may be able to save your reputation yet."

Alison let her eyes well up. Grandmother Diamond hated crying. But a well-timed tear could work wonders. "Not if I get kicked out of school," she sniffed. "Daddy showed me this yesterday." She slid the envelope across the table to her grandmother, who opened it and read the letter. If there was a change in her expression it was too minute for Alison to see. Asking Her Highness for money was something Alison had never done before. She knew it was risky. The strings attached were liable to get tangled – they could even strangle you. She had seen other family members get wrapped up in them before. But she had no choice. She could not give Kelly the satisfaction of seeing her get kicked out of school.

Grandmother Diamond was silent.

"Do you think you could help?" Alison asked. She was careful with the tone of her voice. It couldn't be too bold or too meek.

Tamara Diamond looked at Alison – the only child of her oldest daughter. Her smile was smug. She probably thought she had an ace in the hole. "Of course, dear," she replied, setting her silver fork down next to her plate. "Say no more."

Drying her tears with her napkin, Alison smiled back. It had gone as well as she had dared to hope. For the moment, Grandmother Diamond was holding all of the cash, but she was not holding all of the cards.

Chapter 26

Kelly felt tingly as she strolled down the Stafford halls the next morning. The school was buzzing. *Everyone* was talking about the photo, which *everyone* had seen. Half the student body was using the pic as wallpaper on their mobiles. Alison Rose was the joke of the day.

You can always count on good gossip to spread, Kelly thought. Three minutes of her time had produced hours of payback. Everyone was laughing about Alison and her new friends, the rainbow unicorns. Kelly's work was done and now she could just sit back and watch the damage.

Kelly was still smiling about it on her way to lunch when Unicorn Girl herself came around the corner. Kelly ignored her. She couldn't be seen talking to lowlife. The daggers shooting from Alison's eyes were all the thanks she needed.

At that moment Keith Jared appeared out of nowhere and whinnied, making his finger into a horn and prancing around. In an instant Alison dropped her eyes and trotted down the hall.

Kelly laughed as she headed into the lunchroom. She hit the salad bar and loaded up her tray with greens and cucumbers. She even allowed herself a couple of California rolls. She felt like celebrating.

Carrying her tray to her table, she looked around to see if her cousin had arrived. She hoped to see her huddled in the corner with her loyal shadow, Zoey, looking utterly defeated. But Zoey was sitting at their usual table by herself, eating a grilled veggie sandwich and drinking a Dr Pepper. Alison was nowhere in sight.

She must be hiding, Kelly thought. The unicorn imitation must have really got to her. Kelly shook her head. What a loser.

Just then Chad set his tray down beside Kelly's, and Tom settled into the chair across from her.

"Hey, boys," Kelly said, straightening the collar on Chad's blue polo. She hadn't seen him all morning. Kelly leaned in to give him a kiss on the cheek and felt him stiffen slightly. She pulled back. What was his deal? This had better not be related to Alison and the stupid pool party.

"What's up?" she asked, wishing she could see inside his head.

Chad turned to face her, his eyes full of frustration. "You really don't know?" he asked quietly.

"No, I don't," Kelly said, feeling annoyed.

"The photo?" he said in a low voice. "Of Alison? That was a low blow. Don't you think she has enough to deal with?"

"Why do you care?" Kelly asked. "It's just a prank," she

said defensively. "Besides, you can't seriously feel sorry for Alison after the way she blamed us for the trouble at the pool the other night—"

"I don't know, Kelly," Chad interrupted. Kelly blinked in surprise. Boys never interrupted her. "Seemed like she helped us get out of there pretty unscathed."

"Maybe from where you were standing," Kelly said. "But we still had to leave dripping wet while she got to go inside and have cocoa in the kitchen."

"That's true," Tom agreed with a laugh. "That was a pretty wet ride home. I thought the driver was going to flip when he saw how drenched we were."

Kelly rewarded Tom with a smile, then slipped her hand into Chad's. She had to keep him firmly on her side. "C'mon, don't be mad at me. It was just a joke. If I'd really wanted to be mean to Alison I could have done much worse. Trust me, I know *all* of her secrets."

Chad took a big bite of spaghetti and washed it down with some milk. "I guess you're right," he told Kelly, giving her hand a little squeeze.

Kelly felt relief wash over her. Then anger. She couldn't believe Chad had even *thought* about taking Alison's side in all this. Didn't he realize what a total loser she had become?

"Man, the stuff I could tell you about her if I wanted to. . ." Kelly said coyly. "But then, I guess every family has its deep, dark secrets to hide. Right, Tom?"

Tom's fork clattered down on his tray and he looked up at Kelly. "What are you getting at?" he demanded.

Kelly leaned forward and put on her most sympathetic face. "It's just, I heard about what happened at Zoey's last school. It's so sad. I hope she is getting some help. I never would have pegged her as the type that likes to play with matches."

Tom was speechless. He looked completely taken aback. Chad looked confused. Inside, Kelly was turning cartwheels. She'd obviously scored an even bigger secret than she had realized. *Thank you, Grog!*

"Are you saying my sister is a pyromaniac?" Tom finally asked. His voice was quiet but steely.

"Oh, sorry." Kelly put her hand on Tom's arm across the table. "I thought . . . I thought you knew."

"Knew what?" Tom looked incredulous now.

"That your sister got kicked out of boarding school for setting it on fire," Kelly said, unable to hide the triumph in her voice.

Tom stared at her as if she had just told him his mother had come back to life. He looked across the lunchroom at his sister. Before Kelly could say another word, he was gone.

Chapter 27

One look at the expression on her brother's face and Zoey knew something was up. And it had to be something major for him to be approaching her at school. *What now?* she wondered. It had already been a weird day. First the bad joke Kelly had played on Alison, who she hadn't seen all day. And now her brother. He looked pretty flipped out when he reached the table. Zoey was not in the mood.

"Is it true?" he blurted loudly. "Did you really burn down the school?"

A bunch of kids at the next table turned to look at her. Zoey felt the whole room tilt. Oh, no. Why was Tom bringing this up now? And how did he find out?

"Sit down," Zoey said, trying hard to ignore all the people staring at them. "And be quiet."

Tom didn't sit. "So it's true," he said loudly. "It's actually true." He ran a hand through his hair, and Zoey noticed he was shaking a little.

"Tom, please," Zoey begged. This was going to be all over school by sixth period. "It's not like it sounds. And anyway, who told you?" Stupid question. She looked across the lunchroom at Kelly and the smirk on her snide face. The queen bee had stung again. But who told *her*? And why couldn't she be like other bees and lose her stinger and die after she struck?

Well, a school was not the only thing Zoey could bring down in flames.

She shot up from her seat, brushed past her brother, and positioned herself in Kelly's face. "That's it, Kelly Diamond Reeves," she said, planting her hands on her hips. "Or should I call you cubic zirconium since you're a total fake? You're not fooling anybody – there is nothing real about you. You don't even have real friends." Beside Kelly, Chad shrank back a little and winced.

Kelly's green eyes stared up at her evenly. "Are you kidding?" she hissed. "My popularity is as real as your little habit of playing with fire."

"Which you know nothing about," Zoey said flatly.

"Except that it got you kicked out of at least one boarding school," Kelly shot back. "Really, Zoey, how pathetic."

Zoey stared at Kelly like she was dog poop on the bottom of a new pair of sandals. "You want to talk about pathetic?" she replied evenly. "How about the way you kiss up to your rich grandmother every chance you get? It's a good thing she, for one, can see right through you."

Kelly was silent, but her eyes were full of fury.

"You'd better be careful, Zirconium," Zoey warned.

"When you're knocked off that pedestal of yours it's going to hurt. A lot."

"Oh, I'm so scared," Kelly said, finding her tongue. "I think I'll run home to Mommy." Her blue eyes looked at Zoey tauntingly. "Oh, wait, that was you, wasn't it? What was it, fifth grade? Making you cry was so easy it was pathetic."

So it was Kelly's fault, Zoey thought. Her mind reeled. Of course. Kelly was the mastermind of every cruel, demented trick in the book.

As she looked at Kelly's smug face, Zoey felt confused. Maybe she was going after the wrong fish. But why hadn't Alison stopped her? A real friend would have stood up for her – she knew what had been going on at home, that her mom's depression had been getting worse. That her parents' marriage was falling apart. Of course, Alison couldn't have known that Zoey's mother would be *killed* that night, but still ... Alison had done absolutely nothing to stick up for Zoey in front of Kelly and the other girls. They were both bad news. It was in their blood.

"Hello?" Kelly said snottily, interrupting Zoey's thoughts. "Anybody home?"

While the kids around her laughed, Zoey smiled down at Kelly. "What would you do if you couldn't use your money to buy popularity? You think Chad and my brother hang out with you because they actually like you? Your own family doesn't even like you. I dare you to find a single person who does, Kelly Reeves."

Kelly stared up at her, her mouth hanging open slightly. She looked thoroughly incensed, and Zoey was pretty much done here – why should she waste any more time on Kelly? She was beyond caring about what Kelly – or anyone at Stafford – thought of her.

With a parting glare, Zoey turned and walked back to her table, picked up her tray, dropped it off, and left the lunchroom. The silence she left behind was deafening.

Chapter 28

When the bell rang marking the end of fifth period, Alison shoved her history book into her bag and rushed out of the classroom. She didn't look at anyone or anything. She didn't stop at her locker. She simply headed for the door.

"Hey, Alison. Trotting off to snuggle with your unicorn friends?" a voice asked as she reached the school exit. Alison turned around and found herself looking at some girl she didn't even really know. Tiffany, she thought her name was.

Alison pushed the metal bar on the door. "Actually, no," she replied, stopping just long enough to answer. "I'm just trying to get away from all the swine." Without waiting to see Tiffany's reaction, she opened the door and stepped into the warm autumn air.

Alison wasted no time. If she was going to cut school she'd better not be busted on the front steps. Skipping down them two at a time, she hurried up the block. All morning long she'd put up with taunts and snickers about that stupid photo. At first she'd ignored it. She told herself that if she could handle her mother being in jail and Chad being with

Kelly, she could certainly handle this. But the past couple of weeks had worn her down. She was exhausted, and the picture had proven to be the final straw.

Putting one foot in front of the other, Alison waited for some relief. She'd had to get out of there – had to get somewhere where she could think.

The image of her tear-and-mascara-streaked face and her kiddie sleeping bag flashed in her head. She could see people's faces, mostly taunting but some even worse – pitying. She'd managed to run into Kelly only once – not easy since they had lockers right across from each other. And then there was Chad. . .

The expression in his eyes when he saw her outside maths class was hard to read. Did he look guilty? Sad? Sorry he'd ever known her? She used to feel like she could tell him anything. He used to tell her stuff, too, about his parents fighting. . . He used to trust her and she'd trusted him, too. Fat lot of good that did.

Alison could feel the warm tears streaming down her face and didn't even bother wiping them away. Instead she slumped at the base of a giant oak tree and put her head in her hands. How could she have been so stupid? Getting one up on Kelly only forced her to raise the stakes. The girl knew no mercy. She was barely even human. But Chad. . .

Why had he chosen to be with Kelly instead of her? Why did he go along with humiliating her in front of the whole school?

Because of Kelly, Alison thought miserably. *Nobody can say no to her. I never did.*

A memory flashed in Alison's face. She was six and on a swing. She asked Kelly to give her a push – and, happily, Kelly did. She pushed her off the swing, hard. Alison had got to her feet and run to their grandmother for comfort. But Tamara had only looked at her sternly.

"If you let her push you and do not push her back, you are the fool and you deserve what you get," she'd said. Alison was shocked. Was her grandmother telling her that pushing was OK? She'd always been told that it *wasn't.* Turning around, Alison saw Kelly swinging high in her place, her pale legs pumping hard in the air. The victorious smile on her face said it all.

Alison lifted her head and looked around. She sniffed and wiped her cheeks with her cashmere sleeve. Grandmother Diamond had been right. She couldn't let Kelly get away with this. It was time to push back.

She knew where she had to go and what she had to do. It was a long walk – Grandmother Diamond's mansion wasn't anywhere near the academy. But Alison was getting used to walking. She would walk all day if she had to.

As she headed down the street Alison could feel her anguish lifting. The sun was shining, the sky was bright blue, and a slight breeze helped push her along. By the time she was halfway there she felt positively giddy with the devilishness of her plan. The Diamond inside her sparkled.

It was positively perfect.

As she punched in the code to unlock the gate, Alison hoped Aunt Christine and Grandmother were away for the day or at least busy bickering over lunch together. Walking around to the side of the house, she spotted Aunt Christine sunning herself by the pool in a Versace bikini and Gucci rhinestone shades.

"Poor Aunt Christine," she murmured. "She's so busy perfecting her tan she has no idea there's a thief on the property."

Alison slipped up the walk, through the back door, up the spiral staircase, and into Aunt Christine's room. The diamond earrings were right there on the dresser, waiting for her.

"Hello, beauties," Alison said quietly as she lifted them out of the box and slipped them into her bag. "I really appreciate your willingness to help me out with my little project. . ."

Suddenly Alison heard a noise in the hall. Holding her breath, she closed the box. Then she crossed the room, pressed her back against the wall, and waited.

Silence.

Peeking out into the hall to make sure the coast was clear, Alison darted back out the way she had come in. Twenty-five minutes later she was back at school. As she glided down the hall to her locker, she realized that nobody was looking at her. There were no heckles. *Weird*, Alison thought. It had been a long time since she'd felt invisible. It felt great.

She could see Kelly and Chad out of the corner of her eye as she twirled the combination lock on her locker. They looked . . . tense. Alison smiled. All was not perfect with the golden couple. Then a conversation caught her ear.

"Can you believe that's why she got kicked out of boarding school?" Audra, the class brain, was saying. "Why would someone *do* something like that?"

"I know, right? She's clearly psycho," her friend replied.

Zoey, Alison thought. *They must be talking about Zoey.* She scanned the hall for her only friend. Where was she?

Chapter 29

Zoey sat across the table from Jeremy at Hardwired. They were supposed to be working on geometry, but they were talking instead. And Zoey was having a hard time not noticing how long and beautiful Jeremy's eyelashes were . . . even while she spilled her guts about the confrontation with Kelly at school.

"I just wanted to smack her. She thinks she can say and do whatever she wants. Like, who died and made her queen? The way she gets such a high out of ruining other people's lives. . ." Zoey said, not caring that she was babbling. "I don't understand why people can't see her for who she really is. My brother and Chad follow her around like pathetic little puppy dogs, and she steps all over them. It's sick. She's totally nasty – and evil. And I thought Alison was bad. . ."

"Really?" Jeremy said, raising an eyebrow. "I thought you and Alison were close."

Zoey grimaced. "It's complicated," she said. "Actually, she's kind of my worst enemy. She totally deserted me when I needed her most. It was a long time ago, but. . ."

"Isn't Alison having an incredibly hard time now? I mean, her mother's in jail. And from everything you've been saying, it doesn't sound like things are going so smoothly for her at school, either."

"Yeah, well, it's almost time for her to hit rock bottom," Zoey said.

Jeremy leaned forward. "Seriously, Zoey," he said. "I don't know what you're planning, but Alison needs you as a friend. If you do to her what she and Kelly did to you, are you any better than they are?" He looked at her pointedly, his blue eyes questioning. "And besides, don't you kind of need her, too?"

Zoey flinched. It was true. Alison was her only friend. Not even her own twin brother had backed her up in the lunchroom today.

Jeremy sat back, and Zoey could tell he was waiting for a reply. His gaze made her uncomfortable . . . mostly because she knew he was right. But she'd been consumed with revenge for so long. She couldn't just let it go.

"*She has to run home to Mommy. . .*" Alison's voice echoed in Zoey's head. She closed her eyes. If only she'd been able to. By the time Zoey got home it was too late. There'd been a terrible accident. Her mother was dead. Zoey had been shipped off to boarding school right after the funeral. She'd never even opened the letter Alison sent her there.

Zoey's mobile rang and she glanced down at the number. "It's Alison."

"Take it," Jeremy said.

Zoey flipped open her phone. "Hey," she said, trying to sound casual. "What's up?" She could feel Jeremy's eyes boring into her from across the table, but she kept her gaze on the floor.

"Zoey! I'm so glad you picked up – I needed to hear a friendly voice. I was so upset about the picture Kelly sent out that I left school right before lunch. And I didn't see you when I got back." She paused for a second, but Zoey didn't say anything. "How are you, by the way? Is everything all right?"

Zoey looked across the table at Jeremy, who was still staring at her intently. "Fine, everything's fine," Zoey said quickly. Alison had obviously got wind of the latest Kelly-instigated rumour and was digging for dirt. But Zoey didn't want to talk about it.

"I was hoping we could hang out tonight," Alison said. "Any chance?"

"Tonight? Uh, I'm kind of busy," Zoey said, ignoring Jeremy, who was nodding at her.

Alison got kind of quiet on the other end. Zoey caught herself almost feeling bad for her. Then she remembered that she *wanted* Alison to feel miserable. "OK," Alison finally said. "I guess I'll just see you tomorrow."

Zoey thought fast. Maybe tonight was the perfect time to see Alison. Maybe now was a good time to strike. Before she lost her nerve. "Actually, I'm almost done here. Why don't we meet at my house in half an hour?"

"Great," Alison said, sounding totally relieved. "See you then."

"Then it is," Zoey agreed. She closed her phone with a snap. There was only one question: was she going to turn on her only friend or not?

Half an hour later Zoey opened the door to a smiling Alison. Zoey greeted her coldly, but Alison rushed in and plopped down on the sofa, totally oblivious. "I'm so glad you invited me over," she said. "Today has been awful."

Zoey closed the front door but didn't turn to face Alison right away. Confusion crashed over her like a giant wave. Alison was right, of course. The day *had* been awful – for both of them. Her argument with Tom, her confrontation with Kelly . . . Zoey suddenly felt too exhausted for revenge. She just wanted to sit on the couch with a friend and tell her all about it. And right now, her only friend was Alison.

Zoey felt kind of dazed as she walked over to the sofa and sat down. "Right, the photo," she said. She still wasn't sure what she was going to do. She studied Alison's face, trying to get a read. Alison looked pretty wiped out, too. "Did I see Percy Puppy in that shot?" Zoey thought she had glimpsed Alison's old stuffed dog.

Alison groaned. "Nice, huh? At least *he* looked good," she joked. "I wish Kelly had at least got my good side."

Zoey was impressed by Alison's ability to laugh at the situation. She'd grown up a lot since fifth grade.

"You don't have a bad side, Alison," Zoey said, surprising herself. "But your cousin has two."

Alison looked hard at Zoey. "Yeah, so what happened today?" she asked softly. "I um, I heard some kids talking about a fire. . . And that you and Kelly had a big fight. About why you left boarding school."

Alison trailed off, waiting for Zoey to pick up the story. Zoey hesitated. She had never told anyone what really happened that day.

"We don't have to talk about it," Alison offered. "But I'd like to hear the true story. Not the Kelly Reeves version."

Zoey bit her bottom lip. No one had ever asked for her side of the story. Not the headmaster at school, not her father, not her twin.

Alison studied Zoey's face. "Never mind," she said softly. "Let's talk about something else."

Zoey shook her head. She wanted to talk about it. She wanted to get the whole story out. She wanted Alison to know. She took a deep breath.

"Boarding school was terrible," she said flatly. "All of them. The kids were all evil and perfectly dressed and the teachers thought they were your parents and your principal all rolled into one. I didn't mind the teachers too much at first. After Mom died, Dad could barely stand to look at us, so I kind of needed all the parents I could get."

"Oh, Zoey," Alison said softly.

Zoey kept talking. "The last school I got kicked out of

was the worst. Everyone thought they knew me – that they could put me in some kind of box. But nobody had any idea who I really am, and nobody cared. So I started to cut class, like I did at the other schools. And my grades slipped. Again. And slipped some more. And then, when I heard the dean was looking for me, I holed up in a supply closet in my dorm."

Zoey was talking fast. She knew she had to get it all out before she lost her nerve. "It was great in there. It was the only place I could be by myself where no one could find me. But it was crowded. And I needed some light so I could write in my journal. . . I had a candle. . ." She could feel her eyes begin to water again as the memories came flooding back. The dark closet. The loneliness. She could smell the cleaning supplies. "Before I knew it, the closet was on fire and smoke was pouring into the dorm." She sniffed. "No one was hurt, but . . . I was expelled that same day – my fifth expulsion in four years, so I had to come back to Stafford. And my dad had to pull some serious strings for them to take me."

Zoey wiped her cheek on her sweater and looked over at Alison, half expecting her to laugh. How stupid to start a fire in a supply closet and then blubber about it like a baby.

But Alison was not laughing or sneering. She was looking at Zoey with the saddest expression Zoey had ever seen.

"Oh, Zoey," she said, moving over to hug her. "You must

have been so miserable! How could they not have seen how great you are? I wish I had been there. What a bunch of losers!"

Zoey sniffled again. "Yeah, well, it definitely felt like *I* was the loser."

"Zoey Ramirez, you are not a loser," Alison said firmly. "You are the coolest person I know. You're tough. And funny. And way braver than I am." Alison looked like she really meant it. "Besides, you have a fabulous sense of style and you're the best friend I've ever had."

Alison paused for a second, then went on. "I've been meaning to say. . . Well, I'm so sorry about that night. You know, in fifth grade? I should have backed you up. But Kelly . . . well, there's no excuse, really. You're my friend, and I treated you terribly. And then your mom . . . I didn't know—" Alison gulped. "I'm so sorry."

Alison's eyes welled up as she searched Zoey's face. "I didn't know what was happening until it was too late. I wanted to talk to you at the funeral, but everything was so weird and your dad was acting like a prison guard or something. And then, before I knew it, before I could tell you I was sorry, you were gone."

Zoey looked up. "Like my mom," she said sadly. "Sometimes I still can't believe she's gone, you know?"

All Alison could do was nod dumbly. She wondered how she would feel if her mom were dead instead of in jail. A tear slid down her cheek and she brushed it away impatiently.

She felt like she had been crying for ever. But it felt good to do it for somebody else. "I just wish I could take it back. I wish I could make it better." Alison's blue eyes were sad and sincere and questioning all at once.

Zoey sniffed and leaned over to give Alison a hug. "I wish I could make things better for you, too," Zoey said, squeezing tight.

There was a weird silence while Zoey ran out to grab some tissues. She handed the box to Alison, then cracked a smile. "So how are things otherwise?"

"You really want to know?" Alison asked, hoping she would say yes.

"Of course." Zoey nodded.

"Well, my dad is totally losing it. He's drinking all the time. I'm not even sure if he's going to work any more. And my mom's trial. . . It hasn't started yet, but it's going to be ugly. It sounds like they have a lot of evidence against her."

"Ugh," Zoey said.

"And here's the weirdest part," Alison said, almost in a whisper. "In spite of everything, I kind of like having her in jail. It makes me feel . . . free."

Zoey grimaced. "Now if we could only get Kelly incarcerated. . ."

Alison laughed so hard she felt limp. "Yes," she gasped. "Please. Let's get to work on that."

Chapter 30

Kelly scowled as she pushed open the door to her grandmother's mansion. Yesterday had not gone as well as she had hoped, but today was a complete disaster. Nobody had noticed her new Ya-Ya sweater and skirt – not even Chad, who seemed even more wishy-washy than usual. Alison was already acting like the photo incident had never happened and, even worse, so was the rest of the school. Her cousin was like Teflon – nothing stuck to her. Nobody was talking about Alison any more, and some of the kids were even talking *to* her. Even the Zoey rumour blew over too quickly. It made Kelly's blood boil.

And now, to top it all off, she had to sit through another tedious dinner at Her Highness's palace in honour of Aunt Christine's last night in town. Alison would be there, of course, and everyone would be fawning over Little Miss Perfect. The whole thing made her want to puke.

Kelly stepped into the grand foyer and was nearly accosted by her grandmother. "On time, for a change," Tamara said snidely, waving her gold cane. "Maybe you are finally learning the importance of promptness." She stared at Kelly and leaned slightly on her new unconcealed weapon.

"I didn't want to be late for dinner, of course," Kelly said sweetly. She scanned her grandmother for something she could compliment her on. It had to be just the right thing or she would be accused of brown-nosing. "Is that a new scarf, Grandmother?" she asked sweetly. "It looks lovely with your heather suit."

"Thank you," Tamara replied. Kelly couldn't tell if she had annoyed her or not. Sometimes it was best just to keep quiet.

"Is Aunt Christine here?" Kelly asked.

Tamara nodded. "She's upstairs. She should be down any minute. Your parents are in the parlour, and Alison—"

"Just had a lovely swim in the pool," said a voice from the other end of the hall. Alison came up to them, fully dressed but still shaking the water from her ears. She smiled broadly at Kelly. "Too bad you didn't get here sooner," she said. "The water was absolutely perfect."

Kelly smiled back. *Too bad there wasn't an accidental drowning,* she thought. Alison always was too good a swimmer.

Just then the cook came into the hall to announce that dinner was ready.

"I'll go tell Aunt Christine," Kelly said, taking a step towards the stairs. She was suddenly feeling like her aunt was the closest thing to an ally she was going to see all night.

"No, she'll be down in a moment," Grandmother Diamond said, shaking her head. "Why don't you go tell your parents instead?"

Tamara let Alison take her arm and lead her into the dining room. Kelly could hear them whispering to each other as they exited the hall. Disgusting.

Kelly rushed into the parlour. "Dinner's ready," she called to her parents without even greeting them. Since the pool bust she'd been avoiding them even more than usual. Her mother's permanent look of disappointment was too irritating for words.

Kelly rushed back into the dining room and sat down at her seat. The less alone time Alison and her grandmother had together, the better.

The cook was halfway through serving the soup when Aunt Christine stomped into the dining room, eyes blazing. "My diamond earrings are missing," she announced, her gaze moving from Kelly to Alison and back to Kelly again. "Missing. Gone." She paused for dramatic effect, and then: "Which one of you girls took them?"

Kelly sucked in her breath.

Alison looked innocently across the table at her aunt. "Which diamond earrings?" she asked. "Oh, the ones Kelly said would be perfect with her slinky dress? What did you end up wearing to the dance, Kelly?"

Out of the corner of her eye, Kelly saw her grandmother smile. Or was it a smirk? Either way, it was totally unfair!

"I said they'd look good," Kelly said evenly. "But I'm not the family thief . . . Al."

"Kelly!" her mother cried.

Kelly glared at her and her tightly pursed lips. Didn't she know when to keep quiet?

"What an awful thing to say," Phoebe chastised.

Ignoring her aunt, Alison raised an eyebrow. "Oh, *you* don't have a stealing problem? Did you black out during the part when you stole my boyfriend?"

"Chad is a person with his own free will," Kelly retorted. "You can't steal a person – just things. What's the word for your little problem?" she asked, waving her soup spoon in the air. "Oh, yes, kleptomania."

"Hmmm. . ." Alison replied. "Which do you suppose is worse, kleptomania or egomania?"

"Girls, girls," Grandmother said, raising a hand in the air. She looked oddly amused – and proud. "Enough. We will settle the matter of the missing earrings after dinner. Christine, Kelly will help you look for them. Right now it is time to eat."

Kelly glared across the table at Alison. The matter was going to get settled all right. And how.

Chapter 31

Alison turned off the gold tap and checked her hair in the mirror. Dinner had been ... interesting. She hadn't expected the earrings to come up so fast, or for Aunt Christine to be *so* angry. But she was pleased with the way things had gone. She could tell Grandmother Diamond was on her side, as usual. It was nice to have a powerful ally.

So far, so good, she thought as she opened the door ... and found herself face-to-face with Kelly. *Or not so good*, she corrected herself.

"I know you did this," Kelly hissed, just centimetres from her face.

Alison's heart fluttered. Even here, on home turf and with Grandmother Diamond in her corner, Kelly was scary. She had no mercy, no shame. And she drew no lines.

Alison stared her cousin in the face. She was part of this family. She and Kelly practically had the same blood pumping through their veins. She could take it. And she could dish it out, too.

"You started this war when you stole Chad and humiliated me in front of the entire school," Alison said plainly. "When you abandoned me at my lowest moment, then tried to ruin me . . . just for the fun of it." Her voice was steady, even as her heart pounded in her chest. "But guess what? I'm still standing. Tall, in fact. And when all of this is over, you're going to be the one lying on the ground. You started this war, but you're not going to win it."

Before Kelly could think of something to say, Alison pushed past her cousin and retired to the parlour to have tea with her grandmother.

Chapter 32

Kelly got down on her stomach and searched under the bed for the missing earrings. They weren't there, of course. Alison had probably already sold them to a pawn shop by now.

"They're not here," she grumbled, getting to her feet. She turned to face her aunt, who was brushing her blonde hair and looking at her own reflection in the mirror. "I didn't steal them," Kelly insisted. "You have to believe me. I know it was Alison."

Aunt Christine looked hard at Kelly, then turned back to herself. "I didn't say you did," she said slowly. "But no matter what happened, you managed to put yourself in the middle of this." Her green eyes met Kelly's in the mirror. "You should not have allowed yourself to become the victim. You should have seen this coming."

"But you're the one who accused me!" Kelly replied hotly. "You should have been defending me down there, and instead you watched Alison and me go at it like you were at a tennis match."

Aunt Christine smirked. "Interesting analogy," she said. "It was a pretty good volley, wasn't it?"

Kelly was not amused. "It's not funny!" she bellowed.

Aunt Christine dropped the hairbrush on to the dressing table with a clatter and turned on Kelly. "Stop whining," she ordered. "I don't care if I hurt your feelings or if you looked bad in front of your grandmother. It's *your* job to win her respect, not mine. I simply want those earrings back. They were on loan from a jeweller and they cost a fortune. You have to get them for me."

Kelly stared at her aunt. Was she kidding? "Suppose you tell me how I'm supposed to do that?" she demanded.

"Go make up with your little cousin and find out what she did with them," Aunt Christine said logically.

The word "little" grated on Kelly like nails on a chalkboard. "No," she said flatly.

"Kelly, I need to return those earrings."

"So buy a new pair and give them those," Kelly said simply. "How hard can it be?"

Christine's eyes narrowed and she stepped closer to Kelly. Kelly resisted the urge to take a step back. "I can't afford to," Aunt Christine explained evenly, "because I'm spending half my income supporting your family."

Kelly stared at her aunt. "What do you mean you're supporting my family?"

Aunt Christine just looked at her. "There are many things you don't know, Kelly," she said dismissively.

"Like what?" Kelly demanded. "What don't I know?"

"Plenty," Christine replied. "But I didn't call you up here

to trade secrets. You have to get those earrings back. Apologize to Alison."

Kelly's face was starting to feel warm. She could feel her heart pounding in her chest. "I won't do it," she said flatly.

"Yes, you will."

"No way," Kelly repeated.

Aunt Christine's eyes looked like they were on fire. "You will do this. For me. And for your family."

Kelly stared at her aunt. There was no way she was going to kiss up to Alison. Not now, not ever. "I can't," she said quietly.

"You can and you will," Aunt Christine replied evenly, as if the subject were closed. She had returned to the dressing table stool and was once again brushing her hair.

Kelly wanted to rush forward and rip the yellow tresses out of her aunt's skull. She could already see piles of it lying on the red carpet at their feet. "I won't!" she screamed. "And you can't make me! You're not my mother!"

Aunt Christine turned away from the mirror and looked Kelly dead in the face. "What makes you so sure?" she asked calmly.

Chapter 33

Out in the hallway, Alison almost laughed out loud. She quickly covered her mouth with her hand. She didn't want Kelly and Christine to hear her.

"What does that mean?" Kelly demanded.

"Nothing," Aunt Christine replied softly.

"What do you mean, nothing?" Kelly shouted. "Stop talking in riddles!"

Too bad I can't see her face, Alison thought. *That would be priceless. No, I wish I could have told her myself.*

"Never mind," Aunt Christine replied. "I shouldn't have said anything. It's complicated, Kelly."

"Complicated?" Kelly screamed. "Complicated?"

"Pull yourself together, Kelly," Aunt Christine said sternly. "Do you want the whole house to hear us?"

Alison heard footsteps approaching the door. Quickly she stepped away and hurried noiselessly down the hall. She hated to miss the rest of the conversation, but she didn't want to get caught. Together Aunt Christine and Kelly had the strength of a hurricane.

Alison slowed her pace when she got to the stairs. She'd

guessed Aunt Christine's secret when she'd seen the picture in the photo album, but she'd had no idea Christine would drop the bomb on Kelly. Why now? And who else knew?

Alison tiptoed downstairs, where things were surprisingly quiet. She was looking for Her Highness. She had some questions. The only sounds were of the cook clearing the table. Alison went into the parlour but it was empty. Walking towards the back of the house, she spotted Tamara through one of the picture windows, walking by the pool.

Alison waved but her grandmother didn't see her. She headed for the doors. She was about to call out, but her grandmother disappeared into the pool house.

And then a huge boom thundered through the room. Alison screamed and ducked as debris flew towards the mansion and giant flames shot towards the sky. The entire pool house was on fire!

Alison yanked open the French doors and was jolted by a wave of intense heat.

"Grandmother!" she screamed.

There was no response. And then a second explosion shook the house and a fresh tower of flames erupted from the burning building.

Don't Miss...

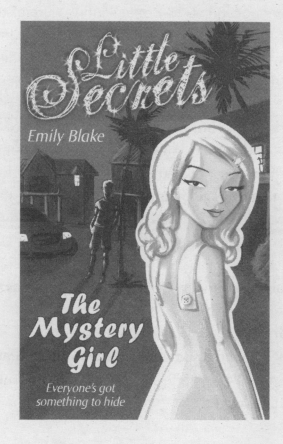

Little Secrets

Emily Blake

The Mystery Girl

Everyone's got something to hide